The Case Files of

GG Michaels

Paranormal Investigator

By J L Meredith

ACKNOWLEDGMENTS

Many thanks to my editor, Christine Hayton

Table of Contents

"Beware; for i am fearless. And therefore powerful."

- Mary Shelly

The Face in the Window

The new school year at Sacred Heart School for Girls was back in full swing. Friendships, interrupted by the summer vacation, were rekindled. The five friends were now officially junior high schoolers.

The night began with a barbecue and music on Mary Beth Murphy's patio. As the sun sank beneath the horizon, the girls moved indoors to watch movies and feast on popcorn. Their choices were romantic movies or scary movies. A vote was taken. Scary won.

Their sleeping bags laid out in front of an enormous TV, the girls gazed up at the flickering screen, spellbound, sometimes dramatically grabbing each other between munching handfuls of popcorn and sipping glasses of juice. There was a lull in the movie about a boy who could see ghosts. The second movie of their planned horror double-feature was about a group of college students who become lost in the woods of Maryland.

Miranda, one of the five, remained hidden under her blanket for much of the time. Guenevere Grace was thirsty from the popcorn's salt and stood up holding her empty glass. She glanced at Miranda, the lump in the sleeping bag. "Guys…don't tease her. Not everyone likes scary movies," Guen said. She smiled while she spoke but felt for her friend's discomfort.

"We will—maybe!" Someone said. The remark drew a chorus of giggles.

"You want some juice, Miranda?"

"Yes, please." A muffled voice came from the sleeping bag.

"Okay, be right back—and you guys just stop!" Guen admonished.

More giggles ensued.

Guenevere paused in the doorway. "I'm changing my vote from horror to rom-com."

"It's still three to two, we win."

Guenevere sighed. "Sorry, Miranda, I tried."

"I know." The tween's muffled voice acknowledged the effort.

"Hurry back, you don't want to miss the end." Mary Beth urged.

"Anyone else want juice?" Guen held up her empty glass for emphasis.

Not bothering to look away from the screen, the three girls responded with a mix of shaking heads and 'no thanks'.

Dressed in cozy flannel pajamas under an equally cozy terrycloth robe, Guenevere wandered off to the kitchen. She listened to the television and noted the tone of the music… nothing exciting was happening. She knew the Murphy household well. She and Mary Beth became friends in kindergarten and when Mrs. Murphy told her years ago to 'make yourself at home' she meant it.

The kitchen was dark and cool. She shivered, tightening the belt of her robe. Retrieving the jug of juice from the refrigerator, Guenevere positioned her glass on the counter under the window, when she spied a white shape outside on the patio. She leaned over the kitchen sink and peered out window for a better look.

In the pool of the patio's light, a teenage girl, sat at the picnic table. She wore a white chemise, and leaned forward, her hands gripping the edge of the table's bench. Her long brown hair obscured her features. Guenevere did not recognize her.

Perplexed, Guenevere turned towards the living room. "Guys! Mrs. Murphy! There's someone out on the patio!"

"What!" Came the reply from one of her friends.

"There's someone—"

"Hurry up! You're going to miss the ending!" Another of her friends cut her off.

Guen's glanced towards in the direction of the stairs, Mrs. Murphy was not responding. "Can you pause it!" she called towards the living room.

"No!" Came the collective reply.

"Can you just..? Oh…" She moaned and frowned, frustrated. "Mrs. Murphy!" She called again, keeping an eye on the girl.

Guen went to the French doors to the patio and tapped on a pane. "Hey…are you alright?" The girl did not look up. Guen's brow furrowed. "Just a sec…"She unlocked the door and pushed on it. It held firm.

Glancing down she noticed why, the deadbolt at the base of the door was set. Giving the girl another glance, she leaned down to unlatch it.

Straightening up, Guen screamed.

Standing at the glass was the girl. Chalk white, her amber eyes flickered with an unholy light. Her blood-red lips drew back into a malevolent, fanged grin. Her hand rested on the door's handle.

Mouth agape, Guenevere stared down at the handle, watching it turn.

The girl's gaze lowered to Guenevere's throat. Her eyes widened. She hissed like an angry cat. Her hands rose to cover her face as if fending off a physical blow. She retreated, shooting the tween a look of pure hate before seeming to run on air into the shadows of the night.

Gasping for breath, Guenevere backed into her friends. They quickly surrounded her.

"Guen!" Mary Beth grabbed her friend by the arms, and looked into her face.

"What's wrong!" Miranda asked.

Heart racing, Guen looked from one's friend to the other. Hyperventilating, she looked towards the doors.

"Guenie?" Mrs. Murphy, pushed her way through the throng, and into her eyes. "Gueny, you're as white as a sheet and shaking like a leaf. Come on, honey," Mrs. Murphy guided her to a chair at the kitchen table, "Just take some deep breaths."

Guenevere nodded, as she was coached through several deep breaths before speaking. "There was someone…" Eyes fluttering Guen pointed towards the door. "…out there."

"Who was it?" Mary Beth asked from behind her mother. Mrs. Murphy, kneeling on the floor to look up at Guenevere, glanced back at her daughter. "Get her a glass of water."

"Who was it Guen?" Mary Beth persisted, ignoring the directive.

"She h-had yellow eyes—" Guenevere stuttered.

"Yellow eyes?" Mrs. Murphy looked at her, bewildered.

"A vampire." Guenevere declared. "She was a vampire. She had—"

"Oh my," Mrs. Murphy gave the girls a stern look. "Just what were you girls watching?"

"No vampire movies, mom. Honest!" Mary Beth glanced from her mother to the doors and back again.

"Listen honey, it was just a bad dream." She smoothed Guenevere's arm before standing up. "You're all shook up. I think it would be best if I called your mom."

"Mom. She wasn't sleeping she was getting a glass of juice."

"There are no such thing as vampires," Mrs. Murphy pronounced. "Now get her a glass of water while I call her mom." Mrs. Murphy left them, pausing to look out into the backyard, and re-lock the door to the patio.

"Guenevere stifled her objection to Mrs. Murphy's assertion.

"What did you see?" Mary Beth asked, handing her friend a glass of juice.

Guenevere accepted the glass and took a swallow before responding. "She had yellow eyes, and red lips, and fangs."She looked from Mary Beth to the others, who in turn looked fearfully at the French doors and the backyard.

"A woman vampire?" Miranda asked.

"But she ran away?" Mary Beth asked.

"I don't know why…" Guenevere said.

"Your cross." Miranda pointed at the tiny silver crucifix hanging from Guenevere's neck. "Your cross scared her away."

Guenevere reached to her neck to touch it. An Easter gift for her confirmation, she rarely took the tiny silver crucifix off.   It had slipped from beneath pajamas. Warmed by her skin, it felt reassuring as her fingers found it.

"I'm gonna go get my rosary." Mary Beth announced.

"Do you have more?" Two of the girls asked simultaneously.

"Yes!" She called back, bounding towards the upstairs and her room.

# # #

Still wearing her pajamas and clutching her rolled up sleeping bag, Guenevere sheltered under her father's protective arm at the Murphy's front door. She listened as the adults discussed things.

"I would appreciate that, in the future, movies of that type were not shown on sleepovers. Guenevere may be a precocious child, but she is still a child." Hal Michaels looked down at his daughter with concern.

Guenevere groaned inwardly but remained quiet.

"You don't have to worry about that, Hal," Mr. Murphy responded, glancing in the direction of the living room, "We're going to be setting the ratings to parental guidance, Mary Beth has enjoyed a few too many privileges when it comes to TV and movies."

"Glad to hear it." Hal said gruffly, before shaking the Murphys' hands and bidding them goodnight.

Guenevere slept in her parent's room, something she had not done since she was an infant. Fiendish yellow eyes haunted her thoughts until exhaustion overtook her. Her mother awakened her a little after eight, handed her a bathrobe and told her she had to come downstairs.

For the next hour Guenevere sat between her parents on the living room sofa while a pair of police detectives carefully asked her about the events of the previous night before. They often asked her the same things, with different phrasing while scribbling onto their notepads as she responded. When they were done, they politely thanked her for her help. Her parents dismissed her, saw the detectives to the door.

Guen ducked around the corner and listened to the conversation.

"Does this have anything to do with the Schaffer girl?" Her dad asked.

Her ears pricked at the name, Schaffer. Everyone in Toledo knew Hannah Schaffer's name. She did not go to Guenevere's school, but her fate was fresh in everyone's mind. Two weeks before school started the fourteen year-old went missing. One week later, her remains were found. The elaborate funeral made the news. She had watched enough movies at Mary Beth's house to know serial killers had a type. The thought she might be the type for whoever killed Hannah, was alarming.

The male detective quickly cut him off. "We really can't comment on an ongoing investigation."

"But you wouldn't be here if you didn't think there was something," Mrs. Michaels reasoned.

The second detective looked at her partner. "They're going to find out on the news anyway."

"What happened?" Mr. Michaels asked.

"Last night there was a homicide about two blocks from the Murphy home," she paused before continuing. "It involved a man walking his dog. The Murphys called us about a potential suspicious person in their yard. Your daughter was the only witness, but her story…"

Guenevere's heart leapt into her throat. Her pulse pounded in her ears. Blinking rapidly, she swallowed and listened intently.

"Our Guinevere is a very honest girl, she didn't make her story up. It could have been someone from her school, jealous about not being invited to the sleepover and they were trying to scare the girls," Mrs. Michaels said.

"It's an elaborate way to get even, but the things they can do with modern makeup…it's possible." The male detective nodded.

"But is Guenevere safe?" Mrs. Michaels persisted.

"I think so but do the common sense things: lock your doors, keep her close to home, call 911 if you see anyone suspicious." The male detective handed his business card to Mr. Michaels before departing.

"That's easy enough." Hal Michaels said.

Frowning, Guenevere darted off for the kitchen's desk top computer. Her parents would not allow her to have her own computer and intentionally placed the family computer in the kitchen. They put parental controls on it for, in their words, her safety. She had to find out more about vampires, and Hannah Schaffer. Her dad entered the kitchen and saw her about to sit down.

"Don't you have a show today, Guenevere?" he asked.

She groaned inwardly, remembering she had to assist her Uncle Henry with a magic show. She loved her Uncle

Henry and liked the fifty dollars it would net her. "At eleven."

"You'd better get your breakfast, and get ready, then. I'll drive you over to Uncle Henry's and he can drop you home afterwards."

# # #

The magic show was uneventful. Uncle Henry, her dad's uncle, and her great-uncle, was a surrogate grandfather to her, and spoiled her like she was his own grandchild. That included treating her to ice cream after the show. They sat in one of the booths at the diner. He wore a bow tie and waistcoat, and she sported a red sequined vest and skirt. They were a little conspicuous.

"Your dad said you had a fright last night," Uncle Henry said between scoops of his chocolate sundae.

"They think I had a nightmare—but I was awake. Why won't anyone believe me?"

"Grown-ups are funny that way, Guenevere," Henry said between spoonfuls of ice cream, "If something is too hard to believe, they make something up that they can believe."

"Harry Houdini believed in—"

"Indeed he did, he didn't find what he was looking for but he believed in—"

"But do you believe me?" Guenevere asked intently.

"I think you saw something, and that you weren't asleep when you did." He jabbed a milky sundae spoon in her direction. "But I want you to listen to your mom and dad, and let the police do their jobs. You're a smart girl. A lot smarter than I was at your age but after what happened to that man and that girl. Stay close to home until they have someone in custody."

"But if she's a—"

"I don't think she is, Guenevere. I think it was someone with a very sick mind trying to scare you girls and that you were lucky."

He changed the subject. "By the way, here's your pay." He reached for his pocket and produced a bill fold. He peeled off fifty dollars in tens and fives, and pushed them across the table to her. "Now you're rich again."

"Thank you." She folded the money and placed it carefully in her tiny purse.

"Now let's get you home, we don't want your mom and dad worrying. You just keep being the good girl that you are."

Guenevere kept her disappointment from her face. "Thank you. And thank you for the ice cream."

"It's always a pleasure." He beamed at her and squeezed her wrist affectionately.

When she arrived home, Guenevere went straight to the computer. Real life encounters with vampires turned out to be people believing they were vampires but were really just humans pretending. The historic remedies for vampires were the same as what was depicted in the scary movies she watched with her friends. For a moment she wondered if her parents were right, and it was some crazy person just playing at being a vampire…but her eyes and teeth seemed so real.

Her search results for the details of Hannah Schaffer's death stood her hair on end and froze her heart.

The girl in the stories was the girl on the patio. The girl with the fangs and yellow eyes, looked exactly like Hannah Schaffer. The only picture they showed was her school picture. The girl in it had jet black hair and enormous blue eyes. Guenevere needed more pictures, and the best place for them was on social media—something the computer's parental controls would not allow. Thinking for a minute, Guenevere fingers danced across the keyboard as she sent an email in a work around to texting.

The subject line to Mary Beth read: 'Can you come over? They won't let me out of the house.'

'You got me cut off from some of the best movies and shows', came the reply.

'I'm sorry but I didn't do that and I didn't ask for it.'

'But I got it.'

The corners of Guenevere lips pressed downward as she typed. 'I'm sorry. I need to borrow your mobile.'

'Why?' Came the terse response.

'That girl that was kidnapped? The girl that was on the patio looked just like her. Only not.'

'Fine. But you'd better not snitch that I let you use it.'

Guenevere's shoulders slumped with relief as she wrote the last message. 'I swear. And sorry again.'

Twenty minutes later, the two girls were in Guenevere's bedroom, poking through Hannah Schaffer's social media. Their access was limited but it was enough.

The two sat side by side on the edge of Guenevere's bed. "That's her, that's totally her." Guenevere said, expanding a picture of Hannah laughing, her expression almost maniacal.

Mary Beth took the phone back and swiped right to advance the photo album. "She's a total Goth, and look at the people she's hanging out with? They look like they're in college." Hannah and her friends were dressed in black and wearing silver jewelry, she looked older than her fourteen years and her friends were at least five years older than her. "Do you think one of them is the vampire that bit her?"

"I'm not sure if vampires show up in pictures." Guenevere wondered aloud.

Mary Beth said, "Probably not. But she's dead Guen, you don't come back from that."

"Unless you're a vampire."

"So what are we supposed to do? Go dig her up and pound a stake into her? Somebody might notice," Mary Beth said incredulously.

"Where was she buried?"

Mary Beth scowled. "I don't know."

"Check the obituaries."

"Just a sec…" Mary Beth's thumbs jabbed at the onscreen keyboard for several seconds.

Guen leaned in to watch as her best friend searched, and found the announcement from the funeral home. Reading it, she groaned and sat back, "Forest Cemetery? That place is huge!"

"What are you going to do? Dig her up?"

"Maybe vampires are like ghosts when they rise from their graves? She wasn't covered in dirt when I saw her."

"*If* it was even her and not some freak pretending to be her. Her friends look like total freaks."

"You don't believe me?" Guenevere asked.

"I'm here aren't I?"

"Thank you." Guen put her arm around Mary Beth to squeeze her shoulders.

"We can't dig her up and we don't even know where she is in that place."

Guenevere leaned forward and pointed to the mobile device. "Maybe there's a map."

"Maybe…" Mary Beth shrugged, and started a new search.

"If we can't dig her up, maybe we could fence her in, you know with crosses or garlic or something?"

Mary Beth shrugged, staring intently at the tiny screen.

Guenevere fidgeted, her heart and mind racing as she watched her friend search.

"It says she's at the family mausoleum in the Old Grounds of the cemetery, section Q13."

"Our lucky number." Guenevere groaned.

"Well if she's in a mausoleum, that would explain why she wasn't covered in dirt. She's buried above ground."

"But those buildings have locks, don't they?"

"Which one of us knows how to pick locks?" Mary Beth dropped her chin to regard her friend intently.

"Lock smith," Guenevere corrected. "And only I learned how so I can do tricks on stage, not to break and enter."

"Well surrounding the place with crosses and garlic is still possible."

"How much do you think we'll need?"

"I don't know, but Uncle Henry paid me for today's show, I can afford a lot of garlic."

"And we could make crosses from popsicle sticks and rubber bands like in that Stephen King movie."

"We? You're going to help!" Feeling a relieved, Guenevere beamed at her friend and hugged her again.

Mary Beth accepted the embrace talking over her friend's shoulder. "Nobody scares the crap of my best friend but me."

Guenevere released her and sat back. "I just thought of something…how do we get there? We can't ride our bikes. It's too far and traffic is crazy."

"Maybe we could take the bus? We have ballet at the club on Monday after school. We could skip out and ride the bus there. Let me check the bus routes." The small screen made tracing the route difficult and required a lot of expanding and reducing the map before it could be planned out. "So it's like four stops… but if they catch us, we're dead."

"If they don't, someone else will be." Guenevere said grimly.

"The police won't believe us, will they?"

"They didn't seem convinced when they came to talk to me this morning."

Mary Beth shrugged. "It's too weird to be believed. I mean, I believe you, but what if it is just someone dressing up to look like her?"

"Well I have a lot of garlic and popsicle sticks then."

"Do you have a lot of them now?"

"We go to brunch after Mass, there's a bodega only a few doors down, I should be able to get everything there."

For two hours they planned, watched videos, read articles, and listened to podcasts. They learned about mausoleums, what weapons they would need, how to use them, and where to find them. They emptied and washed out perfume bottles to fill with holy water at Mass the following morning. They went over the bus route and calculated how long it would take them to find the mausoleum and counted their blessings that it was close to the main gate.

They worked out a story for their dance teacher and for Miranda's mom who would be driving the three of them from school to class. They decided to leave Miranda out of their plans. A call from downstairs signaled Mary Beth's mom had arrived to pick her up.

"Sorry I can't stay over, it's my mom and dad's date night," Mary Beth said, packing up.

"Seriously? After what happened?"

Mary Beth shrugged.

"Well, keep the doors and windows locked and everything." Mary Beth lifted her Rosary from beneath her sweater. "And everything."

"Good." Guenevere blew out a breath. "Call me after dinner."

"Sure, grandma usually falls asleep by eight, anyway." She giggled then her expression became sober as she folded up their list of things to do. "We could get in so much trouble if we get caught."

Guenevere nodded, her own expression sobering. "I know, but like my Uncle Henry said, adults will make up something when they can't believe what they hear. I could tell the police thought I was out of my mind when they left this morning. If they won't believe and help then we have to do it."

"Call you tonight."

Mary Beth's grandma, on instructions from her parents, took her mobile phone away from her at nine o-clock, giving the pair barely an hour of planning before the next day.

Guenevere surreptitiously filled two perfume bottles with holy water from the font in the cathedral's vestibule and raided the sacristy for tablets of incense. She bought garlic at the bodega, explaining to her parents it was part of a school project. In place of popsicle sticks, and at the suggestion of the bodega owner, she bought tongue depressors at a nearby pharmacy.

Much to her chagrin, her parents announced after brunch they were going on a family trip to visit her older sister, Patricia, at Ohio State University in Columbus; a two and a half hour drive each way. By the time they arrived back home, it was well after seven. The sun was rapidly disappearing over the purple and orange horizon. Guenevere felt antsy.

She went straight to the telephone to call Mary Beth, to her surprise, Mrs. Murphy picked up.

"Hello, sweetheart, Mary Beth isn't feeling very well. We think a spider bit her sometime last night and she's had a bad reaction."

Guenevere felt the cold hand of terror seize her heart. The hair on her neck stood on end. Tears welled in her eyes. Her mind raced. "Umm…We're working on a project that's due tomorrow, can I come over and get her part of it?"

"I think that would be okay—but just for a few minutes. She needs to rest."

"Uh-huh, sure. I'll be there right away." She hung up the phone, her mind continuing to race as to what to do.

Her mother was annoyed at having to go out again, and wondered aloud why they hadn't finished their project the day before, drove her to the Murphys'.

Guenevere clutched her school bag to her chest. The ten minute drive was excruciating. Her breath came in short puffs. Her mother wondered if she was feeling alright.

"Just want to make sure that we don't fail."

"Guenevere…" her mother soothed, "You've always done well. Everything will be fine."

Guenevere looked at her mother out of the corner of the eye, hoping her lie remained undetected. She wished she could share her mother's optimism. She wished she could tell her what was going on. She wished none of this had ever happened.

When Mrs. Murphy opened the door, Guenevere barely paused to say hello, before racing past her for the upper storey, taking the stairs two at a time.

"Mary Beth?" Guenevere queried, flinging open the door to her friend's bedroom.

There, perched on the edge of the bed, her mouth stretched open and about to sink her fangs, was Hannah Schaffer.

Her eyes wide, Guenevere gasped and glanced in the direction of the downstairs.

"Scream and I'll tear her open." Hannah lifted a hand tipped with nails that resembled talons. "It's very rude to interrupt someone's dinner, but I forgive you, since you brought dessert." She licked her ruby-red lips with a long pointed tongue. "Now close the door."

Guenevere hesitated.

"Close it." Hannah's hand came to rest on Mary Beth's neck.

Guenevere broke into a cold sweat. Her hand trembled as she reached backwards. Her eyes never leaving Hannah, she pushed at the door until it clicked shut.

"Good, girl." In an instant, Hannah was on her feet and advancing around the bed. "And you dressed for dinner. So pretty."

Staring at her in terror, Guenevere's trembling hand rose to the neck of her dress, to pull the tiny crucifix forth. She held it up between her fingers.

Hannah snarled and retreated. "You and that damn cross!"

Emboldened by the vampire's retreat, Guenevere found her voice. "Get away from her! Leave!"

"For now…" Hannah purred, already halfway out the window. "But I'll see you soon Guenevere…you, your mom, your dad. I'm fun for the whole family." Her amber eyes flashed with malevolence. The laugh that accompanied her threat was unabashedly mocking. She floated off into the night.

Panting, Guenevere vaulted to Mary Beth's side. The girl lay quietly, unaware of the battle that took place just seconds before. Guenevere looked from one side of her neck to the other. On the left side of her neck was a bandage, a purple bruise protruded out from beneath its edges. "Sorry," she apologized pulling it back one side.

At the centre of the bruise were two red dots.

"Hey! Mary Beth!" Guenevere shook her friend. "Wake-up! Shrugging her school bag from her shoulder, Guenevere quickly fished out one of the bottles of holy water. Holding her fingers to the top, she upended it to wet her finger tips and pat holy water onto the wounds.

Steam rose from the injury.

"Hey! Ow!" Mary Beth's face screwed up in pain. She hissed out a breath. Her eyes opened. "Guen?" she asked, her expression puzzled.

"Drink this." Guenevere held the bottle up.

"What is it?"

"Holy water, you've been bitten."

"What?"

"Just drink it. All of it."

Mary Beth gasped. "Hannah?"

"Yes. Now drink it."

"K…" Mary Beth's hand came up to take the bottle. She downed its contents in seconds.

Guenevere watched with astonishment as the red dots faded away.

Mary Beth glanced towards her open window. Tears began to course down her cheeks. "She was here?"

Guenevere embraced her friend. "I got rid of her."

"How did she get in?" Mary Beth sobbed.

"I don't know." Guenevere looked around. "Where can I find a cross?"

"In the hall."

"I'll be right back." Guenevere released her and returned a few seconds later carrying a crucifix.

Mary Beth lay back, watching Guenevere pull the picture off the wall over her bed and hang the crucifix up in its place. "I'm so tired, and so cold." She shivered.

Guenevere closed the window and ensured it was locked. "I'm going to get her MB, I'm gonna stop her. Nobody scares the crap out of my best friend but me." She smiled, what she hoped was an encouraging smile, even though she was terrified.

"We're going to."

"There's no time. Tomorrow, I'm going to get her."

"But—" Mary Beth struggled to sit up.

"You're hurt, and there's no time before she hurts someone else." She heard Hannah's threat echoing in her mind.

"You have to go to the doctor tomorrow. I'm going to send your mom up with some cocoa and marshmallows. She thinks I was here for a school project."

"K…" Mary Beth's breaths became soft and regular as her eyelids slid shut.

Guenevere paused to plant a soft kiss on her friend's forehead and pull the covers up to her chin. She starred out at the night, her jaw set and fury bubbling up within her. "She's not going to hurt anyone ever again."

Taking her rosary from her tiny purse, Guenevere kissed its medal of St. Michael and carefully hung it from the headboard. "Watch over her, please."

# # #

Monday seemed to drag, then speed up all at once. Guenevere vacillated between fury and terror. Curt and impatient, her classmates wondered why she was so short-tempered. She could not tell them and felt both regret for her manners and a profound sense of loneliness.

Too anxious to eat, she went to the school's chapel and prayed to every saint she could think of for help.

When the final bell rang and Miranda's mother picked the girls up for ballet class, her heart was pounding.

Once they arrived, Miranda believed Guen's story that she was feeling sick and was going to call her mom. Miranda gave her a hug and told her she hoped she felt better before hurrying off to class.

Cemeteries unnerved Guenevere, they felt spooky on sunny days, and today was absolutely dreary. The clouds shrouded the warmth and light of the sun. A breeze rustled the leaves overhead and underfoot. Each step towards the gravesite increased her feelings of impending doom.

Aptly named, Forest cemetery contained a small woodlot near its entrance. At its edge, in section Q13, a long grassy swath separated the woods and a line of oaks and beeches. She passed mossy, moldy, weathered gravestones, some leaned on angles. Save for the caretaker mowing the grass, no one came here. The children and grandchildren of the deceased were deceased themselves.

No bright marble mausoleum stood here. Only one building stood out among the graves, a crypt. She paused to gaze at it, her breaths shallow and her heart racing.

Weathered and gray, patches of green moss grew on its walls and roof. The name above its door, bold and prominent, read simply Schaffer. On one side, a stone vase held a wilted bunch of roses, their leaves browned and falling from the thorny stems. The other side displayed a list of the names and dates of those interred, including, at the bottom, the name Hannah Schaffer.

Advancing on it, Guenevere's head turned at every creak of the overhead branches and every crunch of the leaves beneath her feet.

A black wrought iron gate, peeling and rusted, covered its entrance. The sight of a heavy, brass padlock lying broken in the turf, elicited a gasp from her. She took a ragged breath. Beyond the gate, the crypt's heavy plank door yawned open. Clutching her family's largest crucifix, she kept her distance as she circled around to look inside.

A short landing gave way to shadowy stairs leading down into utter darkness.

She berated herself for bringing everything but a flashlight. She pondered leaving to find somewhere to buy one, but dismissed the thought. The day was dark enough, delaying would only make it darker.

She dropped her bag at her feet, opened it and pulled out bag after bag of garlic. According to their plan, she could pen Hannah in with a kind of fence. If vampires hated garlic, maybe it would keep her trapped in there until she could do something else.

She kept her distance and watched the entrance as she moved around the crypt, breaking the garlic bulbs into individual cloves and jamming each, along cross made from the tongue depressors and elastics, into the sod. When she was done there was a complete circle all around the crypt.

Guenevere considered what else she could do. Going inside was suicide. She considered dragging cans of gasoline to the crypt to pour them down the stairs and setting the fuel alight but that had all kinds of complications from getting it there to being arrested. But…there was something she could do.

The sachet of potpourri she brought to conceal the smell of garlic was almost as big as a lunch bag, and contained enough tinder that she was sure it would light the incense tablets. She dug out her mother's long candle lighter and clicked its trigger to produce a flame. She decided to stuff the blessed tablets into the sachet and throw it down into the crypt, hoping the sacred smoke would drive Hannah into the daylight.

As she worked she spied her sister's big hand mirror she brought along. Vampires supposedly hated mirrors. Between it and the crucifix, she figured the two would keep Hannah back if she showed up.

Another thought occurred to her, glancing at the overcast sky she wasn't sure how well it would work, but maybe she could reflect some light inside and see further into the crypt.

Guenevere nearly jumped out of her skin when a purring voice oozed out of the darkness.

"It's so convenient when dinner delivers itself. And do I smell garlic? Did you bring pizza? I know what I want on mine."

Guenevere stood stark still, her body refused to move. She stared into the darkness, straining to see the source of the voice. She white knuckled the mirror and the crucifix.

A pale hand shoved at the gate, it squealed open on rusty hinges. Hannah Schaffer stood in the doorway, a fiendish grin on her face.

"You know I really love being a vampire. I never really cared for the sun, or Him." She extended a finger at the crucifix. "One's too hot the other's too dull. By the way…" she paused to survey the circle of tiny crosses around the crypt. "Garlic doesn't work, and those little crosses? They need to be blessed." She glanced upwards at the canopy of shade trees, and the overcast sky and stepped outside.

"Get back!" Guenevere lifted the cross and the mirror, thrusting them forward like weapons.

"Or you'll do what?" Hannah gloated and thrust her arms upward and outward.

Wind roared through the grassy alley with the force of a hurricane, blowing up leaves and twigs, and snapping branches.

Guenevere struggled to stand, squinting as her hair blew about her face. An overhead branch broke, plummeting down towards her. She screamed and fell backwards. The cross and mirror flew from her hands.

Hannah was upon her.

The vampire pinned Guenevere to the ground. Their faces only inches apart, her eyes blazed with diabolic delight. She grinned hungrily. "Well, well…no cross to save you now…not with it underneath you." She roughly poked at Guenevere's silver chain for emphasis.

Guenevere stared with horror at the fiend atop her. Her breaths came in short, sobbing, gasps. Her mind quailed. "M-m-m—" she stuttered.

"M-m-m." She mocked. "You want your mommy? But mommy's not going to save you now. But we'll see her later. I'll even let you have the first taste. In fact, I'll *insist* on it!"

"N-no…" Guenevere struggled beneath Hannah, her hands pushed against the vampire.

"Yes!" Hannah hissed. She swept the girl's hands away and pressed them above her head, pinning Guenevere's elbows to the ground. "Yes. Yes. Yes!" She laughed and tilted her head back, extending her fangs.

Guenevere groaned. Hannah's grip was like steel. Her arms felt like they were being ground into the turf. The vampire's breath smelt like rotten meat.

Hannah looked down at her, "What a pretty pet you'll make. I might even let you keep that uniform. Just think of how many gullible idiots and sleazy men we will reel in…" she looked up waxing poetic. "It will work perfectly."

Fumbling among the twigs and broken branches, Guenevere's fingers brushed something smooth. *The cross!* Desperate hope seized her.

"Why-why are you doing this?" she stuttered, struggling to get her fingers around the base of it.

"Oh sweetie," Hannah unpinned the girls arms and seized the mirror from Guenevere's fingers. "Do you want to see yourself one last time? It's so weird that these things don't work for us…"

Seeing a sliver of sun peeking through the clouds, Guenevere shouted, "Michael!"

Still holding the mirror up to her face, Hannah's derisive scoff became a screech of pain.

Guenevere screamed in alarm, watching the sun's beams reflect off the mirror and engulf Hannah in flames. She burned as quickly as if she was made of flash paper. In seconds all that remained were flakes of ash and scorched bits of chemise.

Her chest heaving, Guenevere laid amongst the fallen branches. The sunshine felt like a warm blanket. She began to smile, and then laugh.

She stood, a feeling of triumph overtaking her. Her heart soared like an eagle. She stretched out her arms and threw back her head in victory.

Mary Beth was safe, her parents were safe, she was safe—as long as she got home before her parents saw the grass stains on her uniform. Maybe Uncle Henry would drive her to the dry cleaners…

The Padded Cell

Guenevere-Grace Michaels' fascination with the paranormal began at age twelve and only grew stronger with each passing year. One of her heroes, Harry Houdini, spent years debunking paranormal phenomena. For better or worse, she had many encounters with the supernatural. Her experiences led her to working towards a degree in Engineering Anomalies at Princeton.

Halloween was in two days and she and her new roommate, Janet Yamashita approached the site of Pi Kappa Gamma's Halloween party. Even at the auspicious Ivy League school of Princeton, the freshmen dorms were raucous and the pair sought to escape them for a more sedate and studious environment. The Pi Kappa's offered that. They were determined to successfully rush the sorority, even if it meant attending a party in an abandoned mental hospital. Since it opened in the late 1800s, as many as ten thousand people had died in hospital before its closure in the 1980s. For her part, Guen hoped the evening would be unremarkable.

The van's headlights flashed over the Overbrook Asylum's sign. Partly concealed by overgrown hedges, and faded from exposure to the elements, the lettering on the sign was still visible. From the passenger seat, Janet Yamashita grinned and pointed at it with a red lacquered finger tip. "We're here!"

Japanese by heritage, Janet kept her hair in a razor bob. Her stature was petite, but her bearing, formidable. Like her friend she dressed for the party's theme of 'Hefs and Bunnies'.

They wore bunny ears and satin strapless corsets, black tights, and stiletto heels, bowties with dress shirt collars and cuffs. The outfits were completed with white fluffy pom-pom tails. Janet's corset was black, Guenevere wore ruby-red.

Guen eased off the accelerator to turn up the driveway and into parking lot. Conventionally beautiful, she was fair, blonde tresses flowed over bare shoulders. Shutting off the engine, she deposited the key fob in her tiny purse and slung it across her body.

Janet reached for the door's handle and beamed back at her "Ready?"

"Sure."

"What's with you? Don't you feel good?"

"I'm fine."

"You're not creeped out are you? I mean…a place like this? It is your major after all." Janet reasoned.

Guen gave a tiny shake of her head. "I'm fine."

Janet dropped her chin and fixed her with a penetrating stare. "If we're going to get out of the dorms, we need to successfully pledge. Try to be congenial and…you know…bubbly."

Guen paused to look her friend in the face, "Like this?" She tilted her head to the side and her lips parted into a mega-watt smile befitting a movie star. Her sea-green eyes sparkled like the stars in the sky.

"It's scary how good you are at that."

"Years of practice," she said, never allowing her expression to waver for even a split-second. Magic shows, both with her Uncle Henry, and as solo magic act, as well as photo shoots, and television commercials, had honed her ability to turn on emotions instantly.

"Well then, let's see if we can find some more boys to chase you."

Guen sighed. Her shoulders fell and she halted her egress. Cocking her head to one side, she patiently regarded her friend. "Part of the reason why we're here tonight is so that we don't have to deal with all of that—"

Janet shook her head. "So *you* don't have to deal with all of that."

"Janet. I'm sorry. But I'm nice, it's who I am, but I don't ask for all the attention."

"Not in so many words."

Guen's palm rose to her chest. "You're blaming me?"

"You could be a little more discouraging."

Guen sighed. "Some of them are very sweet, and I've only ever had one boyfriend. I'm not…"

Janet's expression softened. "I know, you're not. But—"

"How about this, then? How about we just go wow the sisters, get into the house and the problem will take care of itself?"

"You're the toothpaste girl, go dazzle them." Janet jabbed her chin towards the doors.

"*We'll* go dazzle them."

"Sure." Janet hopped out of the van and headed for the asylum's entrance with Guen quickly catching up.

Their exposed skin goose-pimpled and their heels clicked and scraped on the cracked asphalt as they made their way towards the party. The grounds were overgrown. Tall grasses and weeds, browned by the autumn frosts, pierced the blanket of fallen leaves.

Lips pressed together, Guen gazed at the square, flat-faced building. Its wired-covered windows stared balefully at them for daring to interrupt its brooding dilapidation.

Couples and groups crowded the hospital's double door entrance. The coeds were also dressed as bunnies. Their male counterparts wore smoking jackets and dark pajama bottoms, dress shoes and ascots. A few puffed on pipes containing tobacco or other substances, while the pop music and sounds of laughter wafted from the hospital's interior. The party's revelry competed with the roar of a generator tucked down beside the short concrete stairwell at the entrance.

A pair of enormous doormen, whom they guessed, from their letterman jackets, played for Princeton's football team, sipped beer from red cups, and paused to offer them greetings and appreciative grins.

Passing through the glass doors, the full effects of the party struck them in a cacophonous wave of frivolity and mirth. A DJ, surrounded by speakers, leaned over a laptop computer while his head bobbed to the 'thump-thump-thump' of a catchy beat.

Heavy institutional furniture mixed with administrative furniture like rolling chairs, and gurneys made up the furnishings. In the centre of the lobby, groups of bright young things, dressed for the party's theme, stretched their arms into the air while bouncing and dancing to the music.

A pair of young men raced gurneys down a hall each with a laughing, screaming co-ed bunny on board. The flickering lights of Jack-o-lanterns and candles mixed with the DJ's swirling party lights of red, green, blue, and brilliant yellow. The reception desk became a makeshift bar where a pair of bunnies dispensed beer and mixed drinks.

Janet leaned up to Guen's ear to shout over the din, "What do you want to drink!"

Noting the appreciative looks cast in their direction, Guen kept her smile in place, and dropped her chin to speak into Janet's ear. "Nothing yet! I just want to look around!"

Janet shrugged. "Suit yourself!" She turned to work her way through the throng to the bar.

Guen stepped away from the entrance and moved to where a glass-faced medicine cabinet displayed a selection of flickering, expertly carved, jack-o-lanterns. There was a ghost, a black cat, a witch, along with various carved faces some jovial, others grotesque. She considered the interior of the lobby. A floor that at one time was white was now a dingy shade of beige-grey. The walls were a sickly shade of faded chartreuse. Many had passed through the front doors only to die—many unpleasantly. The Partiers in the centre of the lobby seemed oblivious to it.

A young man, lanky and fit, his hair slicked back, and a flush of red to his face, pulled her from her reflections.

"Hey. I see you peeking, but not speaking." He grinned.

The line forced a tiny giggle and surprised smile. "Hello…" she said, detecting alcohol on his breath.

"I'm Hugh, Hugh Heffner. I'd like to welcome you to my party…" he made a grade sweeping gesture to the revelry.

"Well, Hugh…I'm—"

"Playmate of the Night."

"Just the Night?" She folded her arms across her chest and fixed him with a dubious look.

"Well…if you can dance, maybe the week."

"Maybe a whole week, huh?" She touched her tongue to her upper lip to keep from laughing at the assertion.

"Come on, Bunny, let's dance." He took her hand and pulled her into the crush.

There wasn't a lot of dancing at the Sacred Heart School for Girls. This was a chance to catch-up, even if only for a few moments. The music was catchy, and she gave herself over. Raising her hands in the air in an imitation of the crowd, she danced with him.

She caught sight of Janet holding a drink. Her roommate pointed at her and giggled before shaking her head and turning to venture into a shadowy hallway leading off of the lobby. Guen was about to pursue and caution her about wandering off when 'Hugh' spun her around by her hips.

Still holding her waist, he leaned down to talk into her ear. "We're having an after party at the Alpha-E, and you're invited."

Guen recognized the nickname for the Alpha-Epsilon fraternity and knew their reputation for philandering. "The-" Guen began to politely turn him down when she spied something strange behind him. Her brows rose and her jaw dropped open.

Standing in the corner, shoulders hunched was a young man in his twenties. His straw-colored hair was disheveled. His robe was not a posh smoking jacket, but rather threadbare and faded like it had been washed too often. His feet and legs were bare and his complexion pale. Most startling of all, she could see through him to the wall beyond. He stared back at her, his expression forlorn.

A chill ran down her spine. She gasped and turned abruptly seeking Janet.

"Hey? What's wrong?" Hugh asked, turning her back to him.

"Sorry, I need to find my friend." She explained hurriedly.

"Your boyfriend?" Hugh asked.

Guen shook her head, "No." She cast a glance back in the direction of the figure. He had vanished. Freeing herself from Hugh's grasp, she scurried for the shadowy hallway where Janet disappeared.

"Hey!" Hugh called after her.

"Sorry!" she apologized over her shoulder, wading through the oblivious partiers to enter the darkness of the hallway.

Feeling her heart racing, she called out, "Janet?" Glancing back with irritation at the music's volume, she took a shuddering breath, fished her mobile phone from her purse, and turned on its flashlight.

The phone's brilliance only made the shadows seem darker and deeper. Lifting it she started down the hallway, peering into each room searching for her roommate.

A check of the women's restroom found sorority bunnies three deep in front of the mirror adjusting their makeup and costumes by candlelight. Janet was not among them.

Poking her head into other rooms revealed, private bottle parties, couples canoodling, and a poker game. The gamblers asked her to bring them some beers. She ignored the request and continued her search.

Several doors from the central party, and much to her relief, she found Janet. She was part of a group gathered around a gurney. At its centre was a Ouija board.

She recoiled at the sight.

Janet looked up from the group and smiled in the candle light. "Hey Guen, this should interest you." She waved her inward. "We're playing Ouija. Want in?"

"No. No, thank you." She gave the room an anxious look.

"Why not?" Janet laughed, looking at the others gathered around the board. "It's fun."

Guen gave her an impatient look and motioned her towards the door. "Can I talk to you a minute?"

Janet turned to the group, apologized, and excused herself. "What's wrong?"

"About ten thousand people died in this building. Using one of those things is just asking for trouble." She spared an uneasy glance at the group around the board.

"Oh come on!" Janet scoffed, "Just how do you know that?

"Besides being an engineering anomalies major and these places are what we study," she licked her lips before continuing, "I just saw one."

Janet's brows knit together. "One..? One what?"

Guen glanced at the group and dropped her chin to speak. "A—"

A blood-curdling scream interrupted their chat and caused them to jump fearfully against.

Across the hall and one door down, a male partygoer, pale as a sheet, shot out into the corridor, barefoot and missing his smoking jacket. A look of terror marred his face. He ran past them anxiously cursing a string of expletives.

His flight was immediately followed by a tall brunette, missing her bunny ears and shoes. She was tucking herself back into her corset and screaming hysterically as she ran after him.

The straw-haired figure, with the dingy robe appeared in the center of the corridor. Arms outstretched, he howled as if in agony and streaked after the pair.

As he passed, the two friends pressed themselves to the wall.

The lights went out.

Every candle, every jack-o-lantern, the generator powering the DJ's sound system, even Guen's phone, the entire asylum was as black as pitch.

"Oh my God!" Janet shrieked. "Run!"

Guen pulled her friend into her arms like her older sister would hug her when she was younger and frightened. "Hold on!" She held her fast.

"What are you doing!" Janet struggled angrily.

Struggling to control her own panic, Guen stood still in the blackness. "Wait just a second! Just one second! We can't see anything…you'll trip and get trampled. Let me get a light back on."

"Let me go!" Janet snapped.

Guen lifted her arms to power up her mobile phone, the screen's light dimly illuminated Janet's indignant expression. Janet's eyes flashed. "What the hell?"

"I'm sorry. I just don't want you to get hurt. Do you see that?" Guen found the flashlight option on her phone and pointed it towards the bedlam in the hospital lobby.

Panic had quickly spread through the guests. Shouts and screams resounded as the howling ghost charged through their midst, passing through living bodies and out the other side. Some partiers fell trying to get out of the way, others screamed unable to avoid the ghost's charge. A stampede ensued, and Guen and Janet were soon alone.

"Is he gone?" Janet asked, her face still a mix of emotions.

Guen bit her bottom lip. "No…" she stared down the hall. "Not yet…"

"What do you mean?"

"I saw him earlier, that's what I came to tell you. He's trapped here…he's not where he's supposed to be."

"I know where I want to be."

"Let's go." Guen's started for the lobby.

"Finally!"

The light of the phone guided their steps back to the lobby where a puddle glistened at the periphery of the light.

Janet's face screwed up with disgust. "Ugh…someone puked."

Guen shook her head. She crouched down at the edge of the glistening viscous. "No…it's…not that. It's…" she glanced up at Janet, her expression one of wonder, "It's ectoplasm."

"It's what?" Janet asked irritably.

Guen paused and realized now was not the time for a lengthy explanation. "It's ghost goo."

"Gross."

Guen shrugged and nodded agreeably. "A little."

"Can we get out of here now?" Janet glanced towards the doors.

Guen straightened up.

Janet sighed deeply and her shoulders sagged.

The pair passed by the small crowd lingering at the edge of the parking lot. Cheryl Webster was president of the sorority, chief organizer, and hostess of the party. Her face glistened with ectoplasm. Swaddled in a blanket, she argued with a small clique of her sorority sisters while gesturing at the asylum. She hurled a soaked tissue onto the ground. It impacted with an audible splat. The majority of the party-goers were piling into vehicles to roar out of the parking lot.

Guen walked around to the van's rear while Janet climbed into the passenger seat.

Purchased from wages accrued from appearing in television commercials hawking everything from mascara and shampoo to hosiery and sunblock, the full-sized black van was eminently practical. It transported all the props for her magic shows, occasionally served as a makeshift dressing room, and carried her ever growing supply of paranormal investigation equipment.

"What are you doing?" Janet called as Guen opened the rear doors.

Stripping the rabbit ears from her head and the cuffs from her wrists, Guen opened a large, black leather messenger bag to examine its contents.

"Janet?" Guen asked gently.

Janet gave her roommate a sideways look. "What?"

"I need your help."

"With what?" she asked suspiciously. "And close the doors. It's freaking cold enough in here as it is."

Giving the messenger bag a satisfied glance, Guen picked it up, closed the rear doors and walked around to the driver's side and got in. "I need your help." She looked at Janet.

Janet regarded her roommate warily. "With what?"

"I'm going back in."

Janet's eyes, flew open, her expression was one of bewilderment. "You're what!"

"I need you to come with…" Guen nibbled her bottom lip, her expression one of supplication.

"Have you lost your mind? We're safe here."

"You'll be safe in there too. You've seen the worst he can do. He makes some noise, and he's see-through. It's weird but not—"

Janet dropped her chin and looked Guen in the eye. "Hell no."

"Please?"

"This isn't some lost puppy, or a little kid, Guenevere."

"He was someone's child once and he's trapped…tormented. I just want—"

"And I don't want to be trapped in there with him."

"It won't take long, we just find him, and get him moving on to—"

"*We* need to be moving on home, like them." Janet pointed at cars streaking into the night.

"I know it's scary."

"And, sorry, but stupid. Look…if you want to borrow my toothpaste? Take as much as you want. If you forgot your card and need me to pay at the cafeteria? No problem. But—"

"It's okay, I understand," Guen lowered her eyes and nodded, "A person would have to be crazy to go into a haunted asylum at eleven o'clock at night—"

"At anytime."

"At anytime. And I know this isn't your passion it's mine. So I'll be back as soon as I can." Guen opened her door and exited, striding purposefully towards the asylum, her heels clicking a cadence on the broken asphalt.

Janet sat for a moment, watching her friend walk across the parking lot, headed for the asylum's entrance.

"Damn it!" Frowning, Janet jumped out to pursue her.

"Guen!" she called, "Don't go. It's not safe."

"Where are you going?" Cheryl asked as Guen strode past.

"You're not going back in there, are you? Are you crazy!"

"There's someone still in there." Guen said over her shoulder.

"What? No there isn't!" Cheryl snapped.

Janet jogged after her roommate, giving the clique an embarrassed shrug as she passed them. "What are you doing?" Janet asked, catching up to Guen and her pace. "Do you want to get into the sorority or not? They're gonna think you're a weirdo."

"Wouldn't be the first time." Guen retorted, not missing a step.

"Why are you doing this?" Janet demanded.

"Someone caught in there?" A deep male voice bellowed, interrupting Guen's reply.

The pair of women looked at each other and turned to find out who shouted. One of the two doorman advanced a few steps from the crowd.

"It's alright!" Guen waved him off with a friendly smile. "We'll be back shortly!"

"You sure?" he persisted.

"We're sure." Guen nodded and resumed her trek.

Janet stood on the sidewalk, glancing from the group to her friend. "Oh…hell!" She grumbled and scurried after her roommate.

Janet reached her and Guen beamed at her with affection. "I knew you'd come!"

Janet scowled. "If I die, I'm going to come back and haunt you."

"Deal." Guen smiled and reached into her bag and drew out a long, heavy black flashlight. "All I need you to do is hold the flashlight."

"Just that?" Janet accepted the light and switched it on to shine it on the asylum's entrance.

"Uh-huh." Guen nodded, "I'll do the rest." Guen dipped back into her bag and withdrew a rosary, its beads clicked softly as she squeezed it in her hand.

"What do you have that for?" Janet asked warily.

"I always pray before I go on a job." Guen said, crossing herself and began to murmur chant-like.

Janet's brows raised in an expression of astonishment. She remained quiet as they mounted the steps and passed through the doors into the comparative warmth of the interior.

Guen finished her prayer. "Thank you again for coming with me, it means so much." She smoothed Janet's bare arm.

"Was that Latin?"

"Yes!" Guenevere smiled brightly, "Eleven years of it."

"So you speak Latin?"

"Yes." Guenevere paused to giggle at her roommate's incredulity.

"For real?"

"It was a requirement for graduation."

"Wow."

Guenevere shrugged good-naturedly and began to rummage through her bag to find her Mel meter.

"What's that?" Janet asked, leaning in with the light to examine it.

"It's called a Mel meter and it's how we're going to find him. It measures electromagnetic fields and ambient temperatures."

"I hope it works fast."

"Me too." Guen said with a desire greater than her expression revealed.

She lifted her phone shining its light forward and recording while holding the EMF meter in her opposite hand. Peering into the darkness with trepidation, she took a deep breath.

"Let's go…" she started to walk in the direction the ghost moved earlier.

"So this is what you usually do when…you…you know, ghost-bust?" Janet asked, gripping the flashlight tightly.

Guen glanced from her devices with mild amusement. "Usually? Yes."

"Was this one…usual?"

"The class one fully interactive apparition?"

"Sure…" Janet glanced around apprehensively

Guen checked the meter and kept her concern from her face. The lack of electricity in the building would normally register as zero but the meter was already registering. She felt like she was swimming in shark infested waters at night.

"You would be surprised how common they are, but the

one we're looking for is probably in one of the wards. We'll start with the closest one, right down there." She pointed down the corridor to an abandoned nursing station next to an archway missing its double doors.

Janet stayed beside Guenevere, shining the light into each of the patient rooms. Outside of each room, a patient board indicated its number and the first names of the occupants. Most rooms were wards with four heavy-framed beds, some still retaining their vinyl covered mattresses. The walls were covered in dingy mint-green tiles and dusty privacy curtains hung from the ceilings.

"Anything?" Janet asked, looking down at the meter.

Guen felt a chill brush along the back of her neck. She licked her lips and swept the meter up and down, watching for the needle to spike and for the registration of a cold spot. The atmosphere felt thick and the temperature was dropping.

A closed door pushed the needle past the mid-point. Guen glanced at her friend and looked down at the meter.

"Here?" Janet asked.

"Maybe..." She drew closer to the door, the meter measured no change in temperature but the needle swung hard to the right, like a speeding car's speedometer. "Probably. Hopefully it's him."

"Hopefully?"

"It's not calibrated to a specific..." she paused searching for a simpler term. "Energy."

"Okay? So what happens next?"

Stuffing the meter back into her bag, Guenevere plucked a stainless steel flask from an internal sheath.

Janet's eyes lit up. "Oh Good. I'm thirsty too. Can I get a drink when you're done?"

Guenevere snickered, rolled her eyes good-naturedly and shook her head. "This is an aspersorium. It holds holy water—triple blessed holy water from Madonna del Pozzo in Rome."

"Okay, well if that's the best." Janet shrugged, regarding the polished bottle curiously.

"It is." Guenevere paused to unscrew the top. Ingeniously engineered, the top formed the base of an aspergillum. Resembling a tiny perforated mace, it glistened with its contents.

"Why do you have this?"

"It helps with…trouble." The blonde turned to face the door.

Janet watched as Guen held up the aspergillum and began to flick it first vertically, then horizontally on the door while murmuring a prayer. The perforated ball atop the stick sprinkled the flask's contents across it like droplets of silver.

"And that helps?"

"It doesn't hurt—at least not us, but hold onto this just in case." Guen thrust the flask into Janet's free hand.

Janet took a moment to regard the steel bottle, while its contents sloshed within. "Okay…"

"Ready?"

Janet blinked. "It's safe, right?"

"I'm just going to get him home."

"And if he doesn't want to go?"

"I've never had one who didn't."

Janet's brows rose. "Okay."

"It's going to be all right." Guen gave her a nod and a reassuring smile and read the name on the room's patient board. "Marv…" she murmured and nodded.

The door swung inward to a padded room. The walls and floor were stained a shade of grey and beige from wear and time. Standing in the doorway, Guen gazed upwards. Lacey cobwebs stretched across the upper corners. She stepped inside and felt her shoe's heel poke through the padded floor.

She stepped back and out of her shoes. "I don't want to get stuck in the floor," she said in response to Janet's look of question.

"Are you sure about this? I mean…anyone they put in here would be…you know…a little…"

Feeling a sudden sense of unease after Janet's implied observation, she took a shallow breath. "Sure…" She nodded. "It'll be fine." Guenevere squared her shoulders. "I just need you to stand there and shine the light into the room while I call him."

Guen stepped into the room. She glanced down feeling her feet sink into the padded floor. "Marv?" she called out tentatively, pondering what she would need to do if the invitation into the light didn't work. It would involve a hammer and an iron nail to bind him to the room and the use of blessed salt around its perimeter to keep him from wandering, long enough for her to call in extra help.

"Marv? Marvin? First, I want to apologize for the party. No one wanted to bother you…" Her voice trailed off. She glanced back at Janet.

The door slammed shut, its deadbolt locking with a click.

Adrenaline shot through Guen's veins. She spun around frantically, searching for the source she could feel but not see. She went to the door, her fingers tracing its jamb by her phone's light.

There was no handle.

A marrow-chilling cold filled the room. She shivered. The hair on the back of her neck stood on end. Her breath came out as tiny white puffs. The cold at her back was like ice. Slowly she turned.

"Guen!" Janet shouted through the door, her voice heavily muffled by the padding.

Heart racing, Guen swallowed the lump in her throat. "Marvin?" Gathering her courage, she straightened up.

Janet pounded on the door, and heaved on its handle. The door's lock would not budge. She called to her friend again.

"I'm here!" Guen shouted to Janet. "He's here…" she said much more quietly.

Her throat suddenly dry, Guen took a shuddering breath. "Marvin. I'm going to pray for you so you can go home…"

"Guen! I'm going to get help!" Janet took off down the hall, her footfalls echoing through the emptiness.

Guen remained in place, certain he was immediately in front of her. Licking her lips, she crossed herself and began to pray a prayer of deliverance, "Lux aeterna luceat eis, Domine, cum sanctis tuis in aeternum, quia pius es. Requiem aeternam dona eis Domine, et lux perpetua luceat eis. Kyrie, eleison. Christe, eleison. Kyrie, eleison. Amen." Crossing herself again, she stood watching and listening.

A breeze as soft as a sigh brushed past her. The bone-chilling cold ceased. She bowed her head to whisper a prayer and Janet burst into the room. The football player, who offered to help, followed behind her.

"Guen!" Janet threw her arms around her, squeezing her into an embrace. "Are you alright?"

"You good?" the athlete asked, his immense size filling the doorway. He leaned one arm on the jamb, a flashlight in his opposite hand.

Janet released Guen, smiled, and half turned to gesture to him. "That's Izaak. He was already coming down the hall to help."

A low, menacing growl, interrupted their celebration.

Guen's heart leapt into her throat.

"What was that?" Janet looked around frantically.

"Trouble. Run!" Guen grabbed Janet's wrist and started for the door.

Izaak flew backwards and smashed against the wall across the corridor.

The padded room's door slammed shut.

A wind with the force of a hurricane whipped through the place, knocking the pair of women to the floor. The flashlight and aspersorium flew from Janet's grasp. The stench of vomit, excrement, rotting garbage, and sulphur filled the air.

On her hands and knees and crawling for the flashlight, Janet's hand rose to cover her nose and mouth. "Oh my God…" she groaned.

"There is no God here…only me…" a voice rasped mockingly.

"It lies!" Guen snapped impulsively.

Guen flew from the floor, grunting as she thumped against the wall, the wind knocked from her. Limbs outstretched, she struggled, wriggling against a seemingly giant hand. It pressed her to the wall from neck to knees and all the way out to her elbows.

"You took from me." The voice hissed before becoming a seductive purr. "But I have something for you…"

Janet began to regain her feet, starring up at Guen with bewilderment. "Guen?" she asked in trembling voice.

"Don't…" Continuing to struggle, Guen grunted through gritted teeth, "Talk to it."

"Silence!" The entity roared like a lion.

The slap turned Guen's head. Her chin fell to her chest. She struggled to remain conscious as black dots filled her vision. "You want them to look at you the way they look at her. You can have as many as you want. I can give that to you." The entity rasped to Janet.

"He…lies…" Guen managed to rasp out a response before she screamed.

Long red scratches appeared on Guen's fair flesh. Beginning at her neck they travelled downward, shredding her costume.

"Guen!" Janet screamed.

A heavy thump could be heard against the door.

Guen groaned, teeth gritted, she called for help. "God, come to my assistance. Lord, make haste to help me." Guen choked, as the pressure on her form, mashed her into the wall's thick padding.

She wheezed out a cough.

"He can't help you." The voice jeered.

Guen gurgled, feeling her strength ebbing, "He…he," she coughed again. "…drew me from the deadly pit, from the miry clay. He…He set my feet…He set my feet upon a rock—"

The unstoppered aspersorium flew through the air, its contents sloshing outward in a splash against what pressed Guen into the wall.

The flask's contents seemed to boil in mid-air. There was a roar and a hiss, like a bucket of water being poured out onto a bonfire. A full-throated, howl of pain erupted. The building shook violently.

In the low light of the fallen flashlight a vague, winged shape flickered into view. Horned, and covered in blackened scales, its fanged maw tipped back in anguish as it clawed the air and then vanished in a cloud of stinking sulphur.

Guen fell to the floor with a thump. Janet frantically crawled to her side, as Izaak burst into the room.

"Guen?" Janet asked, beginning to roll her over.

Guen looked at her numbly, it was as if Janet was shouting down at her through water.

"I've got her." Izaak stripped off his coat and stooped to wrap it around her form before plucking her up and cradling her in his arms. "Let's go!" he shouted turning for the door in a sprint.

Grabbing the fallen flashlight and Guen's phone, Janet followed.

A terrible tumult of venomous blasphemies and tortured wails filled the asylum. The cacophony chilled their blood and set their teeth on edge, chasing them all the way to the exit.

Out on the sidewalk, a group of sheriff's deputies advanced. They halted at the appearance of the trio.

"She needs the paramedics," Izaak said. He brushed past them and headed for the flashing lights of the emergency vehicles in the parking lot.

Guen groaned. Her ears continued to ring. She looked into his face and saw the concern there. "Thank you. I'll be okay."

"You will be in a minute." Izaak said, his long strides determined and unrelenting.

"I need my phone." She looked back at the building.

"Why?" Izaak asked.

Trotting alongside them, Janet handed it to her. "Here…"

Guen's thumbs danced across the screen until she found what she was looking for. Staring at the screen, she began to murmur softly before ending with an audible 'amen'. She handed the phone back to Janet. "Pray this."

"What?"

"It's a prayer of binding. We don't want them following us home."

"Seriously?" Janet asked.

Guenevere looked at her with disbelief. "After all of that?"

"Right." Janet took the phone and began reciting the unfamiliar words.

"You too, Izaak" Guen instructed and smiled at him.

"Sure thing." He gently lowered her into the care of the paramedics. They took into the back of the ambulance and pulled the doors shut.

# # #

Sitting in the van's passenger seat, Janet looked up from her accounting textbook and looked out at the asylum. "How long do these things take?"

Her scratches and bruised jaw healed, Guen regarded her friend patiently. "They have to bless every room, exorcise it and hold a Requiem Mass—a Mass for the dead. So…until they're done." Guen responded from the driver's seat. She glanced at her phone, they arrived in the parking lot at 8:00 AM. It was almost noon.

The Saturday morning after their ordeal, Guen made an impassioned plea to meet with the bishop of the Trenton diocese. A preliminary meeting with his assistant, and a recount of events, complete with a demonstration of her bandages hidden beneath a turtleneck sweater, led to a meeting with both the bishop and the diocese exorcist.

Two weeks later, after an investigation and arrangements had been made, the bishop, five exorcists, some from neighboring dioceses, another dozen priests and a score of nuns now wandered the halls of the asylum, releasing the souls trapped within and driving out the entities that held them hostage.

"What time is Izaak coming by the house?"

Guen smiled at the thought. "I'm just going to meet him after the game."

"You're going?"

Guen shrugged and smiled, her eyes flashing with mirth.

"Holy!" Janet pointed at the building as a bright light flashed through the windows of the entire facade.

"Looks like they're done." Guen let out a sigh of relief.

"And look who's coming." Janet watched the bishop stride down the sidewalk towards the asylum parking lot.

Guen powered down the window.

The bishop smiled. "I brought your aspersorium and your shoes. The vessel is an interesting and practical invention."

Guen's face brightened accepting the return of her possessions. "Thank you, Your Excellency. My dad made it. He's an engineer."

"Good man. Now who wants pizza?"

She glanced at Janet and shrugged. "Um…sure!"

Ouroboros' Charm

"That's it…" Guenevere Grace Michaels glanced over at her roommate as she drove. She watched the gleaming silver dollar roll up onto the back of her finger, and seemingly disappear. "Perfect! You got it!" Guen grinned with pride. Janet's training in coin tricks had taken weeks, but Guen found it fun to watch her progress. Just as her Great Uncle Henry enjoyed teaching her the fundamentals of stage magic when she was ten.

She was happy to have something else to discuss rather than the 'Ouroboros' Conglomerate' and their collection of industries of fertilizer, perfumes, and adult pharmaceuticals. Janet, being a business and commerce major at Princeton, seemed to be able to talk endlessly about it.

"Will you stop hounding me now?" Janet Yamashita asked, her tone one of exasperation, but her smile filled with the pride of accomplishment. She switched the coin into her opposite hand to flex and stretch her fingers.

"Oh come on…" Guen scoffed. "Your fingers are stronger than mine."

"This isn't grabbing and throwing people around. This is—
"

"Are you admitting—"

"No, I'm just saying—"

"Uh-huh." Guen giggled and noted the GPS on her phone. Glancing in the rearview mirror, Guen took her foot off the accelerator, gently applied the brakes, and rolled the panel van to a stop on the highway's gravel shoulder.

"Why are we stopping?" Janet craned her neck, looking for the source of their journey's interruption.

"There's a henge around here, on a ley line." Guen pulled her panel van onto the shoulder of the rural highway.

Guen's magic shows, and appearances in print and television advertisements hawking everything from shampoo and toothpaste to sunblock and hosiery, had paid for it.

The van served as transportation for all of her props, her investigation equipment, and occasionally, as an improvised dressing room.

"Jargon." Janet responded, watching Guen power down the driver's side window and take a powerful flashlight from her bag and shine it on the field across the road, tracing it all the way across to a distant hillock and a wood lot.

Pretty and Japanese by heritage, Janet and Guen's were roommates in their freshman year at Princeton. Now out of the dormitories, they remained roommates, and made up two of the three partners in Guen's paranormal detective business, GG Michaels Investigations.

Guen sighed to herself. "Remember when I talked about it—"

"You talk about a lot of weird things. You have to tell me when it's an important weird thing."

"Remember when I talked about Stone Henge?"

"In England?"

"Well you remembered that part."

Janet rolled her eyes. "What about the stone henge?"

"Henges? Circles of stones? They're all over Britain, Ireland, and Europe. Not so much in the US, but there's one around here. Druids used them for their rituals."

"And?"

"They're normally five-thousand years old, but sometime after Europeans arrived this one appeared. It's just—"

"Weird."

Guen glanced at Janet with mild frustration. "Unusual."

"What is that smell?"

"Soil, the Kilpatricks said the soil is so rich that they have the best food in the whole south-east."

"I'm from San Francisco, the only soil we have comes in flower pots, and it doesn't stink."

"It's sweet…full of life."

"Well I'm full of coffee, let's get going, I need to pee."

Guen sighed, and gave the wood lot one final look before pulling back onto the highway. "Alright, but I'm going to ask the Kilpatricks if they know where it is. I want to see it."

"Whatever blows your hair back." Janet settled back in her seat.

They passed the town limits sign. It read:

Welcome to Ouroboros' Charm

Founded 1725

Population: 2200

North Carolina's Garden Community

& Home of the Ouroboros Group

They passed beneath Victorian-style streetlamps adorned with green banners stenciled with gold Celtic themes, and did not see a single modern home. Many were Kansas-style apron homes from the first half of the last century, featuring broad, manicured lawns and expansive gardens. Almost every home flew the flags of both America and Ireland. After a few blocks, large Georgian and Victorian homes becoming the norm.

Reading the GPS on her mobile device, Janet directed Guen's driving until they pulled up to a particularly impressive white Victorian home with gingerbread trim. It stood threes stories high, with a turreted corner. Rose buds were already forming on the trellis along its façade. A pair of Range Rovers were parked in a driveway that stretched to the back of the property. "Ritzy." Janet commented, looking up at the house as they parked in front.

"Well, I did meet them at a pretty ritzy soirée in Charlotte."

"That was the weekend…"

"The weekend you abandoned me for romance." Guen sniffed in mock injury.

"Had to be done, Allan has needs—and it was Valentine's."

"*His* needs?" Guen gave her friend sideways look of suspicion.

"His…ours…whatever." Janet shrugged.

"Three nights a week and Valentine's was on a Thursday, the show was Saturday."

"And I'm going to miss our Sunday matinee since you dragged me ten hours from his arms."

"Had to be done. Money is money, even if this is a weird one."

"They're all weird. But are *they* weird? I mean…" Janet looked at the house warily.

"I'm weird."

"A little weird. Not major-league weird. Anyway, I brought grandfather's helper."

Guen sighed.

"What?" Janet asked, perplexed.

"We're here to do simple investigations for their Chamber of Commerce and attend their May Day festival, not hunt monsters."

"You made me get all these special bullets and we never use them."

"I don't think we'll be meeting any vampires or werewolves."

"What about the Irish harp on the lamppost's banner? There could be goblins or leprechauns around." Janet gripped the van's dashboard and leaned forward to warily peer through the windshield before relenting and breaking into a grin.

"That's fairies and cold iron. Now stop teasing me."

"I'm just saying…if they're weird."

"Don't be silly, the Kilpatricks rescued me from the weird ones…"

"It's not weird that men want to get with you. It's weird you won't oblige them."

"Izaak—" Guen began to protest.

"I know, you've said it a thousand times, romance and marriage—"

"Is not a matinee."

"Okay, whatever…when are you going to bring it up?"

"When the moment is right," she headed off Janet's next question. "I don't know when that will be, but I will."

"Okay…" Janet said skeptically.

"I will! Now don't be surly."

"I'm not surly, I'm a polished professional. I even wore this outfit for the entire drive to meet them." She looked down at her clothing, a gray cashmere sweater matched with a black mini-skirt, tights, and flats. Pretty and petite, Janet kept her raven-black hair in a collar-length bob.

"And it is appreciated," Guen said. Blessed with movie-star good looks, Guen was green-eyed, and fair, with waves of blonde tresses that reached her shoulders. She wore a navy-blue pinafore with matching Mary Janes paired with a white turtle neck and tights. A gift from her grandmother, a tiny silver crucifix, hung around her neck. She deduced the Kilpatricks, being Irish, were most likely Catholic and would appreciate that she was too.

The third member of GG Investigations, Izaak Washington, the starting left guard for Princeton's football team, and Guen's boyfriend, was attending a bachelor party for one of his coaches and not along for this contract. Retrieving their bags from the back of the van, they ascended the stairs to the front porch and rang the bell.

"I'm so excited!" Guen gushed.

The light in the front hall flicked on, backlighting two figures through the door's curtain. It opened to a middle-aged couple; a tall, heavy-set man with white hair and a florid complexion, and a handsome silver-haired woman, wearing a flowery silk blouse. "There she is! The queen herself!" They said in sync "And with a lovely lady in waiting," Seamus added. The couple beamed looking from Guen to Janet and back again.

"Mr. and Mrs.—" Guen began to speak.

"Come now, my heart," the woman said in a thick Irish brogue. "Not Mr. and Mrs. Kilpatrick! Maeve and Seamus!" Guen apologized good-naturedly and introduced Janet to them.

"Well come in! Come in!" Speaking in a North Carolina accent, Seamus motioned them forward. "Take your shoes off. Make yourself at home." He relieved the women of their luggage, carrying it inside.

"Lady in waiting?" Janet murmured to Guen. "I'm a lady right now."

"Don't be surly," Guen admonished in a sotto voice while never losing her smile.

"Yes, your highness-ness." Janet rolled her eyes.

The scent of fresh baked bread wafted from the house's interior as the couple ushered them into the front hallway. A vase of fresh tulips rested on a doily atop a chest of drawers next to a hat tree. On the wall adjacent to the door a hung pair of hand carved masks, of Melpomene and Thalia, tragedy and comedy.

They were led into the dining room at the center of the house. A tea service, Charcuterie board of havarti cheese and slices of apple, soda bread and a dish of strawberry marmalade, joined a carafe of brown apple cider.

"How was your drive? Can we offer you some refreshments?"

"We saw a lot of the East coast," Guen said neutrally, glancing at Janet.

"May I use your restroom?" she asked, looking at their hosts.

Maeve pointed to the staircase leading off the dining room. "Certainly, my heart. It's right up the stairs, on the right, next to your room."

With a 'thank you' Janet took her bag from the floor and trotted up the stairs.

"We drank a lot of coffee on the way here," Guen supplied helpfully.

"Ah, yes." Maeve nodded. "Well what can we get you?"

"I'm sorry, I'm gaining five pounds just looking at that bread. It smells so good, and I'm so tempted."

"Giving in to temptation can be a good thing—from time to time. One must live." Seamus picked up a piece of soda bread and bit the corner off a slice for emphasis.

"Fie Seamus, you don't have to walk across a stage in front of thousands—"

"Maybe just some apple?" Guen interrupted their disagreement.

"Of course, apple it is." Maeve enthusiastically offered up the Charcuterie board.

"And cider, you have to have some cider." Seamus urged, setting four cups upright and pouring from the carafe.

Guen accepted a cup as it was offered.

"A toast…" Maeve said.

"A toast to bread! Because without bread there'd be no toast!" Seamus offered, lifting his cup and slice of bread in a salute, as the women giggled.

"Rascal!" Maeve touched her cup to theirs and took a sip.

"Would you care for it toasted, Guen?" Seamus offered thoughtfully.

The cider was lovely, sweet and tangy all at once. Guen wished she could down the entire cup but obliged them with a sip. "It all looks so delicious but I think just the apple slices…" She picked one up and sampled the soft white flesh, it was ambrosia. She quickly finished it and reached for another, murmuring with appreciation as it practically melted on her tongue.

"From our orchard in the backyard." Maeve supplied with an air of pride.

"Well I'm going to make toast." Seamus selected a second slice of soda bread and disappeared into the kitchen off the dining room.

"Would you like to see it? The dress I mean?"

Guen's eyes lit up.

"Come on." Maeve motioned for Guen to follow, leading the way to a side room with pocket doors. She pulled them open to reveal an artisan's studio. One side was a work table furnished with spools of ribbon, straps of leather, a rack of tiny drawers, and a combination lamp and magnifying glass on a flexible arm, on its opposite was a sewing shop, complete with cutting table, sewing machine, several irons, and racks of thread, needles and scissors. What drew Guen's attention was an exquisite gown adorning a dress form. White and sleeveless, with a high neck and slits up both legs to the top of the hips, it hugged the mannequin like a sheathe.

Maeve stood alongside the gown. "What do you think?"

Guen's breath caught, she starred at it, mystified. "It's…it's gorgeous…"

"Thank you. I did my best with the measurements you provided."

Guen crept forward. "May I touch it?" Guen lifted her clean hand for emphasis.

"Of course, Princess Guenevere." Maeve smiled puckishly. Guen caressed the front of the dress's skirt that narrowed to a hand-width sized strip at the floor. It was so soft. "Is this silk?"

"Yes it is!" Maeve beamed. "All natural fabrics," she paused to retrieve a box from a shelf above her sewing table to display a pair of mules made from wood and leather and adorned with silver buckles. "Even your tights are silk."

Guen's hand rose to her throat. "I'm overwhelmed. Thank you so much."

"Nothing but the best for our May Queen. We even have a horse-drawn carriage arranged for the parade."

Guen imagined being at the front of the town's May Day parade. "Again, I am overwhelmed."

"You know your speech?"

"I could do it in my sleep."

"I knew we picked the right girl."

"What about tomorrow? Everyone is ready for us?" Guen asked.

"Twelve sites all ready for investigation. Everyone hopes all of them are haunted."

"They do? Most people are relieved when we tell them it's an electrical problem or a draft."

"The Samhain ghost walk depends upon it. They want your expertly provided proof."

Guen decided not to press the issue. She would speak with property owners individually about the nature and circumstances of ghosts.

"Those are some amazing masks, upstairs in the hall," Janet interrupted them, reappearing at the foot of stairs.

Maeve turned her attention to Janet. "Aren't they though? Mr. Kilpatrick is quite a skilled wood worker. It's one of the ways he likes to relax."

"But not my favorite." Seamus approached the women from behind. Balancing a piece of toast in one hand, he used its opposite to hug his wife's waist and grin.

Maeve snuggled back against her husband. "Behave my mister, we have guests."

"Impossible with such a beautiful wife." Seamus leaned down to kiss his wife's neck and elicit a girlish laugh from her.

"They are so cute," Guen murmured to Janet.

Janet nodded, doing her best to suppress a yawn, before apologizing.

Maeve sobered. "Poor dears, you must be exhausted. We can talk more over breakfast."

Guen helped herself to one more slice of apple and another sip of cider before following their hosts upstairs to their rooms.

# # #

Over a breakfast of yogurt, fruit, eggs, and half a croissant, they decided they would divide the list of hauntings and investigate them in pairs. Janet and Seamus took half of the list while Guen and Maeve took the remainder. It was not until they were on the sidewalk that Guen realized Maeve intended their visits would be made on foot. She instantly regretted wearing her favorite pair of red pumps. The shoes matched the pleated skirt that swished about her knees, but not the task.

Maeve gifted her one of her creations, a white leather choker with an Ouroboros charm. The serpent swallowing its tail represented an ancient symbol of life, death, rebirth, and unity. Guen removed her tiny crucifix to accommodate the gift. A smaller version of the charm on a slender silver chain adorned her ankle. It shone and glimmered against the artificial tan of her stockings.

A sweet chorus of high-pitched chirping filled the mild morning air. "Listen to the birds." Maeve smiled, looking up at the trees that covered the street on both sides in a newly greening canopy. "They're quite frisky this time of year."

"It is spring." Guen agreed. "And it's so pretty here." She gestured to the blooming tulips and daffodils in the gardens up and down the street.

"Well we knew you were coming and made sure to decorate." Maeve's eyes flashed playfully. She reached up to pluck a delicate, white, dogwood bloom from an overhead branch and gave it a sniff.

Guen chuckled at the implication. "I forgot to say thank you for the bath last night, I wasn't expecting it."

"Nonsense, a princess deserves the royal treatment."

"I'm not really a princess, I'm just…"

"You're not just anything. You are our guest and you will experience all Ouroboros' Charm has to offer. A May Queen deserves only the finest hospitality."

"If someone had told me I would do a show and all of this would happen…"

"It was kismet, princess. We were discussing a ghost walk as an added attraction to the Samhain festivities and there you were."

"Well, you two did help me too."

"I expect you know how to handle yourself when it comes to such things."

"It was still very nice of you," she held up her hands to make air quotes, "*Aunt Maeve.*"

"Your *Uncle Seamus* and I were delighted to do it and we are so glad you accepted the invitation to be May Queen."

"Not that I'm not flattered, but when I researched it, I'm older than traditional May Queens."

"Ah, yes." Maeve sighed. "When an ancient tradition meets the influence of such a young country of prom queens, homecoming queens, and Miss Americas, our May Queen tradition bowed to the culture." She shrugged.

"So not everyone in town is Irish?" Guen teased.

"I think there's a foreigner or two from America about but they're the exception." Maeve teased and slipped a hand into the crook of Guen's elbow.

"About Ireland and the town's heritage?"

"Yes?"

"I've read there's a henge in the county?"

"Oh yes, Fàinne an Dia. It's up on the Callaghan farm."

"I think we passed it on our way into town, or at least the wood it's in?"

"Yes, you would have. It's a nice place to go for a ride."

"Oh, I love horses."

Maeve giggled.

Guen looked at her with question.

"The fillies and stallions up there are more of the two-legged sort, my heart."

"Oh?" Guen's eyes flitted from side to side pondering the veiled revelation. "Oh!"

"You are such a sweet girl!" Maeve took Guen's hand to pat it. "Never gone for a—listen to me, such a quidnunc! It's none of my affair."

Guen nodded in acknowledgement. "We haven't. I won't say that we're proud about that, but we're not ashamed of valuing romance and marriage for...*that*. But doesn't the farmer mind?"

"You're an example for us all and I don't think Mr. Callaghan minds, in fact...I think that's where his sons got their beginnings!" Maeve chuckled.

"Oh my!" Guen's brows raised.

"It's a beautiful place, and very romantic. I'll be sure to make sure you see it. You have to leave tomorrow afternoon for home, we'll slip away a little early and I'll take the two of you up there. Most people will be in the park so there shouldn't be too many...riders."

# # #

They strolled through the neighborhood, exchanging greetings with neighbors out walking, gardening, or mowing their lawns. Maeve went over the next day's agenda with Guen, beginning with a parade that led to the park in the center of town. There, she would be crowned and give a speech. Guen admitted she was nervous her address. The

May Pole dance followed. The afternoon events included gathering flowers, a bag-piping competition, Irish stepdancing, a rugby match, and a festival of foods prepared by all the restaurants and confectioners in Ouroboros' Charm.

The pastoral nature of the town quickened as when their steps turned onto the main street. A slight breeze swayed the branches of the red maples, beeches, and oaks lining the thoroughfare on both sides. Guen noted the mistletoe growing in the upper branches. Amorous couples, young and old walked hand in hand or arm in arm, their colognes and perfumes competing with the scents of the vibrant blooms overflowing the streetscape's flower boxes. The perfumes were sweet but not cloying, the colognes, captivating. Guen struggled not to stop and take a second sniff of some of them. She wondered if the factory had an outlet store.

Cars and SUVs, most of European manufacture, cruised past them at a leisurely pace, while others filled the parking spaces next to the cobblestone sidewalks. Green banners stenciled with gold ouroboros, hares, harps, eggs, and mistletoe, hung from the Victorian lamp posts. None of the rural towns and villages of Ohio resembled Ouroboros' Charm. Affluence was on display wherever she looked.

"I have to ask you, what about church? Does everyone skip church for this?"

"No one seems to mind—or at least hasn't said they do." Maeve smiled mildly.

Guen kept her disapproval to herself. She did not like missing Mass. She would have to add it to her next confession before Mass, Tuesday evening.

Maeve stopped at a storefront. They were at their first haunted site. A store converted into the town's movie theatre.

Mr. Ryan, the theatre's plump and balding proprietor, unlocked the glass door and welcomed them. He wore spectacles and a blue blazer. Exchanging pleasantries with the women, he lingered in his gaze and handshake with Guen. Releasing her hand, he explained why he believed the place was haunted.

Guen took the extended greeting in stride, men tended to linger in their gazes wherever she encountered them.

"It's the funniest thing…" he explained, leading them behind the candy counter to the projection booth. "We think old Charlie Kelly, who owned the theatre before me, haunts us. The lights sometimes come up mid-show, especially if the movie is a long one, sometimes the projector will shut itself off. It usually happens if we're showing something for grown-ups." He winked.

Guen blinked and kept her feelings of distaste from her expression. She agreed with Charlie. "All right, umm, has there been any violence? Things flying across the room? Physical attacks like scratching or hitting?"

He shook his head. "Oh no-no-no, nothing like that." Recalling her conversation with Janet the previous night, she decided it was now or never to bring up her issue with this contract. "I could help him move along—if it is him. It's really quite simple—"

"Oh no-no-no." Ryan shook his head, and his jowls, "He's good for business."

"Mr. Ryan, ghosts are souls in purgatory, asking to be let out, to move on to heaven."

"Oh I don't know about that. I think if he wanted to leave, he would."

"How do you determine if there's a ghost here? A séance?" Maeve interrupted.

"Oh I never engage in those, you never know who or what you're talking to. There are lots of liars and imposters, out there in the ether. I use science." She opened the flap of her bag to withdraw an EMF meter. "This will tell me if there are any inexplicable electromagnetic fields or cold spots in the vicinity. But I will need to turn off the power." Her eyes fell upon the circuit breaker box behind Ryan.

"Well, we have flashlights." He picked one up from the projector room desk, flicked it on, and pulled the lever for the main breaker, powering down the entire theater. Holding her meter in one hand and using a thermal camera with the other, she moved through the projector room, and out into the lobby. The electromagnetic field in the direction of the office increased with each step.

"Is there anyone else here with you, Mr. Ryan?" Guen asked over her shoulder. "Any other employees?"

"Oh no-no-no." He shook his head.

Guen entered the office door way. It was a fairly typical space, a desk and a desk top computer, a bulletin board with schedules and important telephone numbers, a pair of filing cabinets, and curiously behind the desk, a small space heater.

Guen watched as the EMF meter's needle moved all the way to the right and the thermal image on the camera showed a rough blue outline at the desk. Her skin goose-pimpled. "I found him."

The pair leaned in on either side, looking from her instruments to the desk and back again.

"That's why it gets chilly in the office. Old Charlie is sitting at my desk!" Mr. Ryan huffed.

"I would say he's trying to get your attention."

"Well he has it!" Ryan exclaimed.

"This is perfect, my heart!" Maeve squeezed Guen's arm enthusiastically. "Kismet!"

"It's what?" Ryan asked, glancing from the instruments to Maeve.

"You're fine with this, Mr. Ryan?" Guen asked, hoping he would relent and allow her to move the ghost on.

"Better than fine, this is fantastic!" Ryan clasped his hands together and grinned.

Guen grimaced.

"Well it seems we have our first verified haunting!" Maeve exclaimed. "You're off to a great start."

"Great job!" Ryan enthused.

"I'm glad I could…find him for you." Guen switched off her instruments and replaced them in their custom fitted sheathes inside her bag. "You can turn the power back on."

Ryan shook her hand. "I'm very grateful."

"We'll be off then," Maeve announced. "Lots more to visit."

"Good luck, see you soon." He smiled at the pair.

Maeve led Guen back out onto the street.

She blinked at the sudden brightness of the morning sun. Maeve gave her a look of reproach. "About your offer to Mr. Ryan…to end the haunting…"

"It's only ethical, most people do not want—"

"The members of the Chamber are not most people. Money, my girl. It's about money. We need you to be a treasure hunter, not an exterminator. The more we can offer to our town's visitors, the more revenue we generate. Do you understand?"

It seemed exploitive to her. She could cancel the contract and return the retainer, but there was her reputation, both for her investigative service and, since Maeve was well acquainted with her stage career, it could be jeopardized as well. The notion of *not finding* any other ghosts, despite her instruments readings occurred to her. The dishonesty of it rankled her ethics and professionalism. Guen nodded, "I understand."

"Good! Let's get going. We have five more to investigate," Maeve paused to check her watch, "And it's already almost ten o'clock."

After a brief stop at the florist to try on the tiara that would become her crown of flowers, white orchids she discovered to her astonishment, their steps led them to the Ouroboros' Charm Opera House. Pushing through its revolving glass doors, the house manager greeted them affably and provided a history of the opera house's haunting. A pair of performers who promised to return to the theatre after their marriage and honeymoon died in an automobile accident in 1924. For the witnesses of disembodied whisperings, phantom clapping, and a pair of floating lights seen moving through the backstage of the theatre, it seemed the couple had kept their promise.

Guen set to work.

With the power turned off, and working by flashlight, Guen's trek led her through the lobby, the opera house's bar, and its offices, before continuing into the opera house itself. It was a sizeable space for a town so small. It featured gilded molding, magnificent frescos, opera boxes and an orchestra pit.

In whispered tones, Maeve proudly explained that the town frequently invited the symphonies and ballet companies of Charlotte and Raleigh to perform at their small venue.

Guen scoured the theatre. She moved from the house to the backstage, under the stage, into the opera boxes, up to the fly tower and down into the dressing rooms. She heard Maeve promoting her skills as a stage illusionist, helpfully suggesting they book her as a future act. Guen harbored mixed feelings about the idea.

After two hours, Guen found multiple areas throughout the theatre with suspicious cold spots and electromagnetic fields that set her meter's needle bouncing. She believed they were being followed by the phantom couple. She declared the theater was, to the delight of Maeve and the house manager, haunted.

Famished and tired from walking for three hours, Maeve treated Guen to a meal at Hearth and Hare, a traditional Irish pub where she was received as visiting royalty. Her salad and roasted chicken breast were so delectable she skipped the dressing and devoured them plain. Afterwards, Maeve invited her to a treat at the boutique chocolatier across the street from the pub.

"Thank you. I have to wear that dress and well…" Guen looked longingly at the chocolate eggs, hares, and maypoles on display in the shop's window. She guessed there was probably more sugar in the larger ones than she normally ate in six months.

"I think I left my noggin back in the pub." Maeve looked to the sky and shook her head. "Do you mind if I…" she glanced at the shop's window.

Guen gestured to the window. "Of course not! Enjoy."
"I'll just get a small treat," Maeve promised before going into the shop, its overhead bell tinkling to announce her arrival.

Guen smiled and took a seat on the bench in front of the shop. The fragrance of the flower box behind it filled her nostrils. She crossed her legs and tugged the pleats of her skirt as close to her knee as the fabric would allow. From her perch she saw Maeve join the queue to be served.

From behind her, Guen heard. Thump-thump. Thump-thump. A sudden stirring scent of cologne caressed her nostrils. She felt her heart quicken and her skin flush. Her hand rose to her throat. She dropped it to her knee, placing her other hand on top.

In her peripheral vision, two figures appeared. They climbed over the planter to join her on either side. Tall, muscular, African in heritage and brutish in size, they wore identical Green rugby shirts that bulged over their considerable musculature. One had cornrows pulled tightly to his scalp the other kept his hair short. Both had neatly trimmed goatees.

"Who have we here, brother?" One said in a thick Irish accent.

"Who indeed, brother?"

She felt their broad shoulders bump against her slender frame. Guen glanced from one to the other in astonishment. Her breath quickened. She quickly realized they were twins.

The one with the cornrows thumped his chest with an enormous hand. "Dajaun."

His brother did likewise. "Badrick."

She was accustomed to male attention, but never had two men literally dropped down beside her. Glancing from one to the others, she responded. "Umm..Guenevere Grace, or Gigi for short."

"Do you prefer long…" Badrick began.

"Or short?" Dajaun completed his sentence.

"It doesn't matter."

"Ah, she's a sweet one, brother." Badrick cooed.

"Doesn't like to hurt a man's feelings." Dajaun nodded.

Guen's brows rose.

"Did we make your heart skip a beat?" Badrick asked.

"Well…" Guen began to respond.

"It's normal." Dajaun affirmed.

Incredulous, Guen giggled nervously. "Okay…where did you two—"

"Come from?" Badrick interrupted.

"Yes." Guen glanced over her shoulder.

"It's where we're going." Dajaun's eyes gleamed.

"And umm…" Guen anxiously licked her lips. "Where is that?" She felt herself struggling to get her bearings.

"A drink." Badrick turned towards her, resting his elbow on the back of the bench.

Dajaun mirrored his brother. "How do you like your wine? Singular or plural?"

"I…" she looked from one to the other. "Don't drink." Her breath came in a pant.

"Today is the perfect day to start." Badrick suggested.

"We recommend plural." Dajaun grinned.

Guen's smile became silly and lopsided. "Plural…?"

"We know the perfect place." Badrick said.

"The Hearth and Hare?" Guen raised her chin over her shoulder towards the pub behind them.

"A more intimate place, Guenevere Grace." Dajaun grinned.

"A place where the nectar is the sweetest." Badrick said.

"And the love is the deepest." Dajaun continued.

"Oh my…" It was one of the smoother invitations she had ever received. Her skin no longer just felt flushed, but fevered. "You two…" She bit her bottom lip.

"Us two." Dajaun's eyes glinted. He covered her folded hands with his much larger one, sliding it up to gently caress the tender flesh just below the hem of her skirt.

"And you." Badrick added, slipping his arm around her shoulders to give her a squeeze.

Guen knew she should stand up and slip free of their familiarity but instead sat blinking in disbelief. The images they were evoking startled her. She could imagine them. She resisted the urge to fan herself, lest it encourage them.

Maeve emerged from the chocolatier. She nibbled on a chocolate egg mounted on a stick like a lollipop.

"Hello gentlemen, I see you've met our beautiful and brilliant May Queen."

"The May Queen?" Badrick withdrew his arm, his expression wide-eyed. "She's beautiful and fair."

"Like no one could compare." Dajaun added, sampling Guen's thigh for one more second before sitting back.

"Indeed the fairest of them all." Maeve smiled, and nibbled another piece off the egg. She munched on it while beaming at Guen, her eyes twinkling.

"I'm jealous." Dajaun's shoulders slumped, his eyes suddenly sad.

Badrick's posture and expression matching his brother's, "I'm crushed."

"So she's a good girl?" Dajaun asked.

"A perfect girl." Badrick grumbled.

"She's a princess," Maeve said.

Guen regarded the three of them. Maeve seemed to be taking too much delight in their disappointment.

Dajaun's expression brightened. "Feel like a ride, Maeve?"

Maeve laughed and advanced upon Dajaun to cup his cheek affectionately. "No-no, not today fellas. You have a match to be hungry for."

"We're famished." Dajaun persisted.

"Damn near starved." Badrick added.

"Talk to me tomorrow, after you win."

Badrick stood up and Guen stifled a gasp at the size of him. He was as big as Izaak, which meant, she quickly learned as Dajaun followed suit, that his brother was as well.

"We will," they declared together.

"See you soon." Badrick's eyes glinted as he looked at Guen.

"By the moon." Dajaun's intense gaze matched his brother's.

"Okay…" Guen gazed at them with a fascination that surprised her. "Bye." She watched them stride down the sidewalk, parting the shoppers as they went.

"Shall we then?" Maeve gestured with her hand.

"Um, sure…" Guen lifted off the bench, her mind filled with questions about the entire encounter, particularly the implications about Maeve and their relationship with the two.

"Feek fellas aren't they?"

"Umm…" Guen regarded her with question. She blinked a few times, their cologne fading but the feelings and thoughts they inspired lingering. She struggled to comprehend her reaction.

"Handsome," Maeve added.

"I guess. I mean…" The attention was flattering, but she had Izaak. If she didn't, their confidence might get one of them a yes, for one of them, but not to hedonism. She was certain she did not want to be the center of that much attention.

"It's alright to notice even if you weren't going to accept their tempting offer."

Guen decided not to press Maeve on her counter proposal. "Do they always speak like that? In rhyming couplets?"

"They work at the fragrance factory but they want to be music rappers—and it isn't the only thing they do in couplets." Maeve giggled.

Oh My. Her head clearing, Guen managed a perfunctory smile as she formulated how quickly she and Janet could make their exit the next day. Janet was right. Maeve *was* weird. The whole town was weird.

"What did they mean by 'under the moon'?"

"I'm not sure. Tomorrow's rugby match—they're our all-star, champion props."

"Props?" Guen asked, imagining a stage.

"It's a rugby position. Big strong fellas up front in the scrum. Their parents are from Jamaica. We enticed them away from Ulster's club and come across and play for Ouroboros' Charm. We haven't lost since they joined."

"Izaak plays left guard for Princeton. He's just as big and strong as them," she said with an air of pride.

"Well I think it was wishful thinking on their part—not that I blame them," she paused to wink at Guen, "By the time of the match though, you'll be up at Fàinne an Dia"

Guen's brows raised.

"Oh, princess. It's fun, it's pleasurable, it's enjoyable, you'll see."

"One day." Guen added.

"One day." Maeve's eyes flashed with mischief.

Maeve led the way to the other locations on Guen's half of the list of haunting. It included the high school where a student drowned and mysterious splashing and thrashing often occurred at night when the pool should be as smooth as glass. There was a Victorian home where a mentally ill woman was kept locked in the attic until her death in the late 1800s. Finally a bank where the manager rejected a teller's romantic overtures and the sounds of sobbing were sometimes heard. Using her instruments, Guen verified that each was most likely, haunted.

"Fancy a bit of sup?" Maeve asked as they completed their final verification.

Maeve's words and behavior had become more conventional after her flirtation in front of the candy shop. Guen was not sure if it was just eccentricity or not, but she agreed to dinner, her stomach demanded food.

Climbing the steps to the front door, Guen noted Seamus' Land Rover was still absent from the driveway.

"I'll give them a call and see what's keeping them before I start supper. Why don't you try on the whole outfit? We can see how it looks and if there is a need for any last minute alterations." Maeve said, as she unlocked the front door to allow them inside.

The backless dress was cut so high on her hips that any sort of under garment was impossible. Her tights had to suffice.

The shoes, size six-b, fit perfectly. Checking her makeup in the studio's mirror, she touched it up for the full effect. Guen looked gorgeous, the dress needed no alterations, it hugged her bust, and abdomen perfectly. She imagined if Izaak saw her, he would lose his mind. The thought of it made her smile. She asked Maeve to use her phone to snap a picture to send to him.

"Certainly!" Maeve came out of the kitchen, drying her hands on a tea towel. She halted in place, gazing at Guen. "Begorrah! You really are a queen."

Guen blushed, lowering her eyes demurely, and murmuring a humble thank you.

Maeve asked her to turn, tugging on, and checking the material. "It looks perfect, how does it feel?"

"Perfect. Thank you." She smiled despite feeling self-conscious.

"Well let's take some pictures."

Maeve took a few, before handing the phone back to Guen. "I talked to Seamus. They've been delayed but will be here by the time I'm done cooking. Would you like a sip of cider while you wait?"

"Thank you, but just a sip." She could drink a quart of the stuff but imagined the sugar content was ridiculous.

"I'll be right back." Maeve strode off.

Guen heard the refrigerator open as she checked the pictures and discovered Maeve's finger had accidently blocked the camera's lens.

"Here you go." Maeve returned bearing a cup of cider to hand to her.

"Sorry, but in all pictures your finger covered the lens." Guen accepted the cup, reflexively taking a sip.

"Oh. I'm sorry, my heart. Can you show me where it is?" Guen took another sip and set the cup down. "Just avoid putting your finger here. She pointed out the phone's camera lens.

"Sorry. Let's try again. Blow him a kiss." Maeve stepped back, waiting for Guen to make the pose, before snapping the picture.

Guen knew how to pose. She began modeling at age 15, which led to doing commercials and even movie parts. She beamed at the camera for a second picture, Izaak would love it!

"Like a bride on her wedding day." Maeve cooed.

"Can I see?" Guen asked.

"Of course, princess." Maeve motioned her over.

Guen took the mobile device from her, flipping from one screen to the other.

The sudden sting in the curve of her right buttock forced a yelp and a jump away from the source of the pain.

Grinning, Maeve held up a syringe, its needle gleamed in the light of the dining room's chandelier.

"What is that! Why…why did you! What did you…." Guen demanded. "Why…" Her vision began to cloud. She struggled to stand, reaching for the back of a chair to steady herself. "Why…" Her question came out as a whisper as her legs began to give way.

"You'll make a beautiful bride for the god. A pleasure and honor awaits you that few ever experience!" Maeve caught Guen's sagging form, grunting as she dragged the younger woman to the adjacent parlor and onto a sofa. "That should keep you for a few hours." She smoothed Guen's hair, before dashing off to her studio for a set of silver manacles. The bonds clacked shut on Guen's wrists. "Too snug for even you to slip free." She smiled and stood up to place a call on her mobile phone. When her husband connected she responded to his questions. "Yes my love, his bride is ready…." She paused to listen. "Yes I'm calling them next…"

# # #

Although she did not possess the breadth of knowledge concerning the paranormal, occult, and mystical that Guen did, Janet could read instruments and relay the findings. She and Seamus began with an historical landmark now closed. The original town courthouse and jail was the site of many hangings.

There they met the county's sheriff, a tall, strapping man with a crew cut and a gold star pinned to his forest green uniform. Gruff in demeanor, he led them through the place stopping at the sites of deaths in the jail and the courtyard where the guilty were hanged. Janet's instruments showed so many possibly haunting that she declared it haunted with complete certainty.

Leaving the jail and the sheriff behind, they continued to confirm hauntings in a tavern, a cemetery, a civil war battlefield, and a farm. Their investigations led them further and further away from Ouroboros' Charm and out into the county.

Janet wondered how far people were going to travel on this 'ghost tour' if they had to do all this driving and verbalized her puzzlement to Seamus as he drove.

"A bus…Janet…a bus. People will buy tickets and we will have two or three buses to move them along. We have to work out a timetable but that would be putting the cart ahead of the horse. We had to confirm with you and Guen's help, we have hauntings for them to experience. Does that make sense?"

She agreed with him and began to continue on with their discussion of Ouroboros' Charm's unique conglomerate of industries. They were number one in profits for organic soil enhancements, perfumes and colognes, and pharmaceuticals to enhance adult desire and libido. Only residents of the county could be shareholders—and only after living in the community for a minimum of five years. If a resident left the county, their shares were bought back by the conglomerate. Given how lucrative the dividends were, it was rare for anyone to leave. Ever the commerce student, Janet found it frustrating, as many did, that the residency requirement kept her from obtaining a piece of their lucrative dividends. In the end, Seamus promised to ask the operations officer to contact her. She beamed with anticipation and gratitude.

Before she knew it, they arrived at their last destination, Ouroboros' Charm's compost and casting factory, Soil Magic.

"This is where the magic happens." Seamus smiled and looked up at the factory's sign as he pulled in to its parking lot and stopped the SUV at the office doors. "Let's go see Mr. Buckley."

Taking her rucksack from the backseat, Janet followed after him, meeting the plant manager at the doors.

A heavyset man with a florid expression and a white hard hat, he wore a sports coat over a golf shirt, Janet guessed Buckley never missed a meal or seconds.

"Sad to say…" he explained leading them down a carpeted corridor to a steel door labeled 'production', "He died when he fell into one of the hoppers we use to grind up compost like leaves and yard waste. Ever since we've had mischief, things shutting down without explanation, lights flickering…things like that. We had the electricians and engineers check things over. They always find nothing wrong, but we have to do a restart every time. He's a nuisance."

Janet touched her nose, stifling a sneeze the smell of the place was like the countryside only far more pungent. "Do you want him removed? I mean, Guen—" Janet began to offer.

"Not at all. Gary's not that much of a nuisance is he?" Seamus asked.

"Not enough to remove him from the tour. Ouroboros' Charm is counting on us to do our part."

"Okay." Janet pressed her lips together. It was part of their investigative service to move ghosts along where possible. Every one of the owners or custodians of the Ouroboros' Charm properties had refused.

"Well…can we get this investigation on the go? We have a wedding tonight." Buckley looked at Janet.

"Oh. I'll get to work. Just show me where the hauntings happen." She looked across the factory with its white tiled walls and its enormous stainless steel bins, hoppers, and wagons.

"I'll show you." Buckley's heavy footfalls rang against the steel steps up to a catwalk ending at an open hopper. Half-full with grass, twigs, and leaves, its stainless steel sides tapered downwards like an inverted pyramid.

"He was leaning over the top when a load of compost was dropped on him and in he went. There was no way to save him." Buckley pointed upward.

Janet set down the rucksack and followed his gaze upwards to a V-shaped bucket that split open at the bottom to deposit its contents.

"Hey! What the hell!" Janet felt herself being hoisted off her feet.

"Sorry honey, you would have made a fine bride too, but I get the feeling your peach has been plucked." Seamus grunted hefting Janet's struggling form towards the hopper. "Damnit Buckley! Give me a hand!"

Janet began her Judo training at age six, continued with karate lessons at age twelve, and completed her self-defense training with every dirty trick her detective grandfather had accumulate in a thirty year policing career. Her instinctual skills sprang to the fore.

Buckley advanced and bent to grab her feet. The sole of Janet's running shoe met his nose. It broke with a crack. Buckley shouted in pain, staggering backwards. His helmet flew off as blood poured from his nose.

"That's enough!" Seamus roared in her ear, a roar that quickly became a yelp of pain.

Janet kicked her heel back and upward, connecting with the fork of Seamus' legs, doubling him over.

Janet felt her feet touch the surface of the grated catwalk, reaching between her legs, she grabbed Seamus' ankle and sat back.

Seamus knee began to hyperextend, he fell onto his back groaning as his body and head met the catwalk's grate.

"You little bitch!" Buckley wiped his hand across his bloody face, pausing to look at it before bellowing and charging her, his head and shoulder lowered in a tackle.

Buckley's head met her abdomen. Bowled backward, she gasped, the wind knocked from her.

"You're going in!" Buckley shouted, lifting her from her feet and pivoting back towards the hopper.

Janet wrapped her legs around his waist, clinging to him as he held her over the hopper. Pressing a forearm across Buckley's throat, Janet grabbed her wrist with her opposite hand and lifted it against his larynx, squeezing it shut.

Buckley choked, releasing her waist to pry at the arms slowly suffocating him.

Janet clung onto him like a lioness bringing down an ailing water buffalo.

He grunted and wheezed swinging his body, and her, to and fro.

She felt him weakening, his legs buckling. Buckley began to stoop. Janet braced her feet against one of the catwalk's white railings and pushed off, ringing Buckley's forehead into the opposite railing.

He fell limp.

Janet dropped to her feet only to confront a recovered Seamus.

"Bitch…I'm going to enjoy this." Jaw set, Seamus' hands balled into fists. Chin lowered, he stalked forward, his face red and eyes filled with hate.

Janet's own hands formed into fists. "You two tubs thought you could get the drop on me!" She thundered. "Kiai!" With three rapid steps, Janet launched herself into the air. Foot extended she caught Seamus square in the face. Seamus' head jerked back, he stumbled, flailing his arms to remain upright.

"You hurt my friend and I'll be the last thing you'll see!" Janet shouted putting on a martial arts clinic, her feet struck his thighs, hips, guts and chest, driving him backwards until he ran out of floor and fell backwards down the stairs. Janet watched him tumble down the steel steps, clattering and banging until he sprawled, unmoving, at the bottom. She paused to glower at him before running to retrieve her pack.

Opening one flap she found her grandfather's revolver and jerked it free. She kept it pointed it at Buckley who remained unconscious. She found her mobile phone and pressed the speed dial for Guen number. "Come on, come on, come on." She murmured feverishly, listening to it ring before getting Guen's cheerful voice message. "Guen!" she shouted into the phone, "These people aren't just crazy, they're psycho! Call me as soon as you get this! I've got Seamus' truck! I'm coming back into town! We have to get the hell out of here!"

Scrambling down the stairs, Janet kept her gun pointed at Seamus as she searched his pockets for his key ring. Finding the fob for the truck, she took off for the parking lot.

Roaring down the highway back towards town, she began to dial 911 for the police and halted herself. If the sheriff was in whatever this group—this cult, was that and was going to this 'wedding' he might try the same thing the two bastards did at the plant.

Her mind raced as to where Guen would be. She refused to entertain the notion they planned to do to Guen what they just tried to do to her. The sun was all but gone below the horizon, stars were already appearing overhead.

A wedding. A white dress. Where… And to who?

The shops and restaurants of Ouroboros' Charm were darkened. Not a single vehicle passed her from either direction. The town had emptied out.

Her heart thundered in her chest. Holding the wheel with one hand, she tracked Guen via her mobile phone. The map led her back to the Kilpatrick home. The driveway was empty Guen's van was parked where they had left it the previous night.

Keys in one hand and the revolver in the other, Janet took the house's steps two at a time. She cursed under her breath, trying several keys before one turned in the lock. Pistol cocked at her hip she entered the darkened house, flipping on lights and straining for a sound. She heard the refrigerator humming in the kitchen.

"Guen!" she shouted, listening for a response and prepared to shoot anyone who got in her way.

Advancing as quickly as she dared she saw the open studio door off the dining room. The white dress was gone. Guen's clothes, her purse, her messenger bag and her phone were all present. "Guen…" she looked around desperately.

She ran upstairs to check their rooms. Their bags were there but the masks were gone from the walls, all of them. Panic setting in, she vacillated. She needed help. The state police could help but she needed a place to send them. Standing in the Kilpatrick's upstairs hall, clutching their luggage, she tried to piece it together.

Where would they hold this damn 'wedding'? They did not seem very churchy, in fact the church next to the cemetery was permanently closed. There did not seem to be any fresh headstones when she was there earlier. Stones… She began to run.

# # #

Ba-Boom. Ba-Boom. Ba-Boom. The drums beat a steady, heart-like cadence.

Guen shivered. Her eyes fluttered open. It was night. The moon seemed fuzzy, outlined by a spiky halo. Her mouth tasted like rubber.

She squeezed her eyes open and closed a few times to clear them. The moon remained out of focus.

What was happening? "Mmam ef maffememm?" Her voice came out muffled. Using her lips, teeth, and tongue, she explored the round rubber blocking her mouth.

She reached to remove it. Her hands could not reach it. "Mhy fan't….?" She mumbled against the gag. She tugged on her arms. Metal pressed into her wrists.

Guen blinked. She knew how to do something about this, but struggled to remember what.

Arching her head, she strained to see what held her. A circle of orange flame, haloed like the moon was all she could see. Staring at it, she wondered what it was as spots danced in front of her eyes.
She heard singing…no…chanting.
Blinking spots from her eyes, she lifted her head to examine her surroundings. There was grass and rocks, tall rocks. She struggled to think, her thoughts mired in a haze before the answer struck her. The henge… The rocks had white circles on them, and white strands of something hung over and between them. Her vision was too fuzzy to make out what it was. What was wrong with her eyes?
She smelled wood smoke, heard crackling and popping, and saw the distorted outline of fires…bonfires. There was movement outside the rocks.
People in white chanted and swayed, their arms extended not upward, but towards the ground.

O Dia mór

Molaimid thú go bhfágann síol

Osclaítear an bláth sin

An tonn féir sin

Molaimid na gaotha a dhéanann cogar

Tríd an leamhán galánta

Tríd an malpais go cruthanta

Tríd an péine bríomhar

Tríd an beithe ag lonrú

Tríd an darach cumhachtach

Molaimid thú as gach ní

Ó athair mór an domhain a thugann beatha.

They completed the chant and began again. It was a language she did not recognize.

What was she lying on? It was soft. It smelled nice. White flowers, so many. They stuck to her back. What was she wearing?

She wore the elegant outfit Maeve created and the silver Ouroboros anklet. It was so pretty…

She jumped and shrieked into the gag when a mask, wooden and richly carved in Celtic knotwork and surrounded by the hood of a white cloak, loomed over her. Two familiar eyes gazed out through its eye holes.

"There, there, princess…there's no jilting the god. Tonight you marry and become one with Daghda," Maeve's soothed in a muffled voice.

Guen's eyes bulged. She cried out against the gag with alarm. "Mham!"

"Relax, your majesty." Maeve stroked her hair. "He'll be here soon enough."

The chanting rose to a fevered pitch as the drums' beat matched Guen's racing heart.

The stone altar trembled. A cheer went up from outside the henge.

The night became silent. Guen glanced up at Maeve. The woman's head was bowed reverently.

Guen lifted her head as high as she could. Something was moving in the darkness. Shifting, squirming, wriggling, coming for her.

"Come, My Lord Daghda! The field is fertile and ready! Your bride awaits!" Maeve lifted a crown of white flowers over her head, and triumphantly placed it atop Gwen's golden tresses.

An earthy, primal cologne filled the air, tantalizing and overwhelming, it beckoned with the promise of delights beyond imagining.

Guen groaned against the gag, as the shadow squirmed into the fires' light.

Barrel-wide and covered in deep-red, fleshy ribs, the enormous worm's conical head came to a rounded, point that swayed from side to side. The heavy flap of flesh covering its mouth, fluttered open and shut, snuffling as its head bounced to and fro, passing through the stone circle towards the altar and Guen.

Wide-eyed, Guen screamed into the gag. She reflexively drew her knees up to her chest.

"Badrick! Dajaun!" Maeve pointed at Guen.

Two heavy bodies in white robes were immediately upon her.

Guen whimpered against the weight and strength of the pair. Groaning against the gag, she felt the big man wedge himself between her waist and her thighs, grunting and forcing her legs down.

His brother surrounded her shins in a bear hug, flipping the shoes off her feet.

"A nervous bride…" Maeve cooed. "There's nothing to be frightened of, my Queen." She ran her a comforting hand over Guen's cheek, tracing her way around to the back of the gown and releasing its clasp at her neck. With both hands, Maeve drew the fabric down, exposing the magnificent, heaving bosom to the murmured delight of the onlooking crowd.

The two men took advantage of the distraction, straightening her legs, and feeding her feet and ankles into the exploring maw.

Guen's breath caught. She felt the fleshy ridges rolling over her feet and ankles, squeezing and contracting, coating her in its fragrant unguent. A sudden euphoria seized her. She stared at the stars gaping with bewilderment.

"She's feeling it brother." Badrick murmured.

"Her first and only." Dajaun said, watching Daghda glide upwards to take hold, and begin a sequence of advances, half-retreats, and pauses, replaying a steady and eternal rhythm with his bride.

Clenching her eyes shut, an expression of bliss seized Guen's features. A flush overtook her fair flesh. Despite the evening's cool, her skin began to glow with perspiration. Maeve clasped her hands together across her breast. Her eyes glistened. "Oh!" she cried. "Oh! He loves you so much! Oh to be loved so! You're giving him more pleasure than you will ever know!" She burst into tears.

Daghda's lips slid up the curve of Guen's calves, squeezing and caressing, savoring his bride's tumultuous bliss.

Guen's body trembled feverishly. Her toes curled inside the worm's silky gob. Her body arched. Stars exploded behind her eyes. "Om! Om! Ommm!" Her ecstatic moans battered the gag.

Maeve unbuckled the leather strap and pulled the white rubber ball from Guen's mouth, freeing her full-throated ecstasy. "Yes! Yes! Yes! Yes my Queen!" Sobbing and weeping, she clasped Guen's hands and gazed down upon the spectacle, joining the assembly in its enthralled murmurs of rapt voyeurism.

Licking her glistening lips, Guen's face screwed up in a grimace of utter bliss, her cries inexhaustible and unbroken. She could see Izaak. It was their wedding night. She loved him so much! Enflamed and bursting with gouts of heat, she gave herself over for consumption…

# # #

Janet pressed the van's accelerator to the floor, flying down the country highway in search of the woodlot. Her hunt was rewarded. Hundreds of vehicles lined the sides of the road in both directions. Janet slowed the van to a crawl to discover the name of a side road before calling the state police. She felt a tiny sense of relief to discover a trooper was in the area and was being dispatched but hung up on the dispatcher when she was advised to remain calm and in place and wait for the officer's arrival.

Heart in her throat, Janet cursed in frustration looking for a road up to the woodlot. She decided to make her own. Finding a large enough space between two parked cars, she rolled through the space, over the shallow ditch, and into the field beyond. She gunned the engine cutting deep ruts into the soil and churning clouds of black dust into the air. She skidded the van to a stop at the edge of the wood, and clambered into its rear. Buckling on her army surplus pistol belt, complete with flashlight, Leatherman tool, and extra speed loaders for her revolver, she slapped on her mining helmet, and grabbed Guen's messenger bag before exiting through the van's rear. In the distance, she saw the rapidly approaching red and blue flashing lights of a police car. Not bothering to wait, she twisted the mining's helmet's light on, drew her pistol, and started into the woods.

She ducked under tree branches and pushed through the undergrowth, cursing at tree roots that conspired to trip her. After many moments she saw a glow through the trees. Shadows shifted and more than once she pointed her weapon at what appeared to be an interdicting sentry but turned out to be a trick of the light.

The smell and crackle of burning wood intermingled with an aroma that reminded her of her lover. Shaking her head to clear it, she heard murmurs of wonder and awe as she drew closer to the flickering glow atop the hillock.

A siren split the night.

The murmurs slowly changed panicked shouts. Brush began to crackle and snap. The sounds of the stampede grew closer. The beams of flashlights pierced the darkness of the woodlot like projector beams in a theater.

Janet ducked behind a broad tree trunk and extinguished her helmet's light. Clutching her gun and wondering if she could shoot someone, her head swiveled from side to side. She watched white-robed figures stream past her, throwing off masks like the ones from the Kilpatrick home. Some runners tripped and fell over branches to be trampled by others. As the siren drew closer, and the mob passed her by, Janet swung out from her hiding place and ran towards the source of the light.

Passing through a cloud of smoke, Janet squinted and gasped at the scene before her.

Guenevere lay atop a stone altar, eyes clenched, head tipped back, about to disappear inside an enormous earth worm.

In the light of a torch, Janet saw a robed figure at Guen's head, holding the blonde's hands.

Assuming a two-handed firing stance, Janet took careful aim and opened fire.

Her aim was true. Six rounds struck the worm's enormous slimy flank.

The god paid the attack no mind, intent upon its joining.

The robed-figure turned, looked at Janet, released Guen's wrists and darted away, moving across the clearing, through the henge and into the woods.

A quick mental survey of the contents of Guen's bag yielded nothing that would stop a hundred yard-long worm. "Hold on, Guen!" Janet yelled, going for the torch.

In a state of adrenalized panic, Janet seized the torch's six-foot stave. She heaved on its polished surface, groaning and cursing while levering it to and fro while eying the worm about to devour her friend. With a final curse of fury it came free. She brandished it in the direction of the monster. "Get away from her!"

Afraid to jam the flames into the worm's flesh lest it rend her friend in its retreat, Janet presented the flaming end close to its side.

The gelatinous covering began to, liquefy and drip. She looked at her friend, dumbfounded by the unabashed moans of pleasure escaping Guen's lips.

Driven back by the torch's heat, Daghda retreated. Guen's glistening, naked body sluiced free of its maw with a sucking sound.

Guen whined plaintively, stretching out her form.

Hearing the thump of running feet, Janet gripped the torch before her to confront the source.

"No, my Lord! Forgive us! I offer myself for your service!" Maeve sprinted from the shadows, tossing her mask and shrugging off her robe to reveal her nude form. She ran after the retreating worm, slipping in its trail of slime, sliding headfirst towards its mouth.

Gripping the torch, Janet watched in fascination and horror as the worm slurped Maeve inside in seconds, punctuating her consumption with a belch while retreating into its hole.

"Guen!" Janet regarded her sobbing and trembling friend. She began to remove her vest before thinking twice and picking up the abandoned robe to cover Guen.

"What…what is happening?" Guen asked groggily. "Where's Izaak?"

"We're going home. That's what's happening." Janet declared. She quickly used her Leatherman tool to jimmy open Guen's manacles, freeing her wrists.

"Izaak…where…?" Guen lifted herself up her elbows and looked around expectantly.

"We'll call him when we get you back to the van."

"No…" she shook her damp tresses, her expression filled with longing. "I saw him. Where is he?"

"Guen…" Janet gazed at her friend with concern. "I think they drugged you."

"I love Izaak, I love him so much Janet! So much! Guen huffed and slowly dragged her hand down her throat to trace her way down her body.

Janet caught Guen's hand. "Okay-okay-okay. I know you do. He's a great guy. Whoa!" Janet's eyes widened. She huffed, her face flushing. "Oh wow!" She licked her lips. A sudden heat in her belly. "That…that's insane." Bending

down she wiped the bit of glistening slime from her hand
on the grass.

"I never knew how much he loved me." Guen panted.
"He…" She erupted into giggles. "I feel so…" She bit her
bottom lip.

Janet nodded hurriedly. "I get the picture. Can you walk?"
Guen sat up, stretching her legs out to touch the cool,
damp of the grass. "What happened? Why am I so…"

"We found a cult of sickos."

"Oh…" Guen nodded.

"We'd better get you looked at." Janet began to help her
slide off the bed of flowers before yanking her hand back
like Guen was like a hot stove. She could feel the heat
radiating off her friend's body.

"You can look right now if you like!" Guen giggled
manically, throwing the robe open.

"No-no-no." Janet shook her head and caught the lapels of
the garment to pull it closed. She glanced around warily.

"Come on, we're going to let the state police handle this
one." She motioned for Guen to slip off the altar.

"Why?" Guen asked, following Janet's direction.

"I'll tell you after we're out of the state and at a hotel."

"I just feel…" Guen bit her bottom lip.

"What?" Janet leaned in, her face filled with concern.

"I feel, I don't know…something. I feel…" she smiled.

"Amazing!" A tremor rocked her body, followed by a full-throated moan. She wobbled, extending her hands to regain her balance.

Janet's brows rose. She frowned and shook her head. "Okay, this is not healthy. We've got to get going." She cast a wary glance in the direction of the worm's hole, anxious it might suddenly return. "Hurry up, come on."

"Sure…" Guen slid off the altar.

Janet walked in silence for several minutes, listening to Guen coo and babble about Izaak's prowess, her utter and complete love for him, and a desire to have his babies. Janet felt a kind of mourning for her friend, to lose the first time joy to a cult's ploy.

They passed scattered wooden masks on the ground near the edge of the woods when Guen halted abruptly and spoke up. "I've been thinking…You were right."

"I was? I mean, I was."

"These people are selfish, and so was I…" She blinked.

"Money isn't a bad thing, Guen."

Guen was silent for a moment, swaying as she walked. She shook her head, "But how you make it matters…" She paused, stared and took a deep breath and sighed it out. "I'm going to say a Novena for the ghosts, and have their names mentioned in the bidding prayers at Mass. This town doesn't seem to understand mercy."

"I don't think we're going to get paid, the Kilpatricks are a couple of psychos."

"Maeve was a little—"

"She's not anything anymore." Janet recalled the image of the woman's rapid suicide.

"What? Why?"

"You don't remember, do you?"

A silly grin appeared on Guen's face. She giggled, shrugged, and shook her head. "Nope, but I feel so good." She dragged out the last word.

Janet allowed herself a split-second of amusement before becoming serious again. "It's probably best that you don't remember." Janet said. "Come on." Janet held the torch before them, lighting the way through the woods.

Beldam and the Belle

Pests. Pests was how his first email described them. Hotelier, Xavier Fox purchased the steamboat the Belle, and he wanted its purported pests…ghosts…removed. Over the past twenty years, other investigators had already found the ghosts. Their motives were fame for themselves and for the vessel. The Belle's resident ghosts were an attraction for the boat-turned period museum and tourist site in the small Kentucky town of Blackwater.
In its nineteenth-century heyday, the Belle moved passengers and cargo along the Ohio and Kentucky rivers before being permanently moored and made into a museum in Blackwater. According to his email and follow-up telephone calls, Fox planned to gut and renovate the vessel before returning to it to service as a hotel, casino, and theatre. The five-hundred dollar advance on her fee lent credence to his intentions.
Fresh from her final examinations in Engineering Anomalies at Princeton University, and now living at her childhood home in Toledo, Ohio, Guenevere Grace Michaels took the contract. Her two partners, Janet Yamashita, her college roommate and best friend of four years, and her boyfriend Izaak Washington of equal time, were home with their families in California and Alabama respectively. They would not be accompanying her on what, to her mind, was a short errand.

Guen began her investigative career at the tender age of twelve. Now in her twenty-second year, her investigations had taken her to   haunted houses, asylums, hospitals, abandoned factories, prisons, overgrown graveyards, forests, and farms. The only thing novel about this job was its location. Moving ghosts along from a property was a simple matter she had undertaken scores of times. Listening to an upbeat Rhythm and Blues tune on the radio, she piloted her black van south towards the village while contemplating her initial research into the Belle's history. According to multiple witnesses, there were three lost souls clinging to the boat, a gambler shot to death in the main saloon for allegedly cheating, a stoker killed by a boiler explosion in the Belle's engine room, and a passenger called Andy Stockton who, in a drunken state, fell overboard and was dragged into the boat's paddles and drowned. There were no reports of violence, but drafts, chills, apparitions, and moved objects were among the phenomenon observed. After five hours of freeways and back roads, she approached the outskirts of the village and her arranged meeting place, a general store called Beldams' Emporium. Constructed of wood with a broad porch and large picture windows, its red and green signage was faded with age. The small parking lot facing the store was empty. She pulled into a space closest to the stairs leading up to its entrance and got out to let out a groan and stretch her hour-glass frame. Changing her shoes from flats to heels, she took her purse and climbed the stairs.

On the porch were rusted tin signs advertising specific brands and goods, many of which no longer existed. An empty rocking chair sat beside a white chest freezer with a blue 'ice' sign. Next to the wooden screen door was a much larger sign describing the store's offerings.

Beldams' Emporium
Antiques

Books

Candy

Coffee

Dry Goods

Fortunes Told

General Merchandise

Ice Cream Sodas

Liquor

Shoe Repair

Stationary

Souvenirs

Tobacco

The 'fortunes told' listing raised her eyebrows. Divination, even done as a novelty, was something she avoided. Some of her cases, those that involved more than a simple haunting, found their origins in the practice of divination. It was a doorway to trouble. She would tell anyone who would listen to leave it closed.

The spring of its outer wooden screen door squeaked and the bell over the interior glass door jingled merrily as she stepped into the emporium's interior. The size of the store and sheer volume of goods struck her immediately. The store was packed from floor to ceiling. Display tables overflowed, shelves were stuffed, and every bit of available space was in use. Her nose wrinkled at the unmistakable and cloying stench of tobacco smoke.

There were racks of road maps and tourist items like hats, t-shirts, and key chains bearing the town's name and the name of its most famous attraction, the Belle. There were post cards, and posters of the riverboat. Toys and riverboat captain hats for children.

Further along there was flatware and kitchen utensils, glasses, cups, and bowls, small appliances like toasters and coffee makers, clocks and transistor radios. Some she did not think were even made anymore. Milk crates of used record albums and a tarnished saxophone, canned goods, light bulbs, and cleaning supplies, the variety astounded her.

She almost crossed herself when her eyes fell upon a beaded curtain, and a white sign decorating its door jamb. The words stenciled in laminated gold paint:

Madam Beldam's Salon

Charms-Cures-Fortunes Told

About to turn away, she startled at a gravelly voice from behind her.

"Sorry to give y'all a start, girl. I'm Mrs. Beldam, Eunice Beldam. This is my place. Y'all lookin' for something in particular? Y'all want your fortune told?"

Guen turned to face the owner of the voice.

Elderly to the point of being venerable, a short, stooped black woman stood in the store's central isle. She wore a navy blue dress with a lace collar. Tight white curls poked from under a roughly woven silk turban. Her brown skin had wrinkled to crags. Puffing on a cigarillo, she wore an affable expression. Bright, youthful eyes peered at Guen with intense curiosity.

Years of performing on stage as a magician as well as acting and modeling trained Guen to change her expressions on a dime. She stifled her alarm, and pasted on a congenial smile. "No…no thank you. I'm supposed to meet someone here."

"Well y'all done just met someone…me." She cackled then took a drag on the cigarillo.

Guen chortled, looking away to roll her eyes in good-natured disbelief. "Yes. I suppose I have…"

Mrs. Beldam jammed a wizened finger at her. "I'll bet yous meetin' a beau. Pretty little thing like you must have lots of beaus."

Guen giggled and shook her head, sending her blonde tresses bouncing about her face and neck. "Thank you but no, I have just one good one, and he's back at his home in Alabama." She smiled at the thought of him.

"Alabama? Y'all don't sound like yous from the South."

"You're right, I'm a Buckeye, born and raised."

"From just up north of here then."

"Yes…and you're from New Orleans?"

"No, La Jolie, it's a little bitty place on the bayou, but still in Louisiana. Can I fix you something at the counter while y'all wait? Pie? Ice cream sundae?"

"Well…" Guen nibbled her bottom lip.

"Where's my head! Y'all want to keep your beau looking at ya. Y'all don't eat sweets. You's probably the kinda girl that takes care of herself. No smoking or drinkin' whisky like me…" She paused to cackle again.

"Right again." Guen simpered.

"Well I is a fortune teller." Mrs. Beldam waggled her fingers in a gesture of mesmerism, and cackled again as she dropped her hands to her sides.

"Maybe just a ginger ale?" Guen offered.

"I can fix that for you." Eunice motioned for her to follow and glanced back over her shoulder as she spoke. "The reason I thought you was meetin' a man is on account of how you's dressed. Pretty blouse and skirt, stockings and heels, I thought for sure you was meetin' a beau. I use to dress that way for my husband back when we was courtin' and sparkin"

Guen stifled a giggle at the terminology and followed her. "My Ernest would have liked you," she said, toddling along to her destination. "He always had an eye for the pretty ones. That's him there, next to me," she pointed a wizened finger at a black and white picture above a collection of pots and pans hanging from hooks above stacks of children's clothing.

Guen paused to exam the picture of a prim looking couple, by the fashion she guessed it had been taken at the time of World War Two, maybe before. Brawny, Ernest wore a black suit, and she, a light colored dress. They were an attractive couple, albeit a bit stolid in their expressions. Mrs. Beldam found her way around to the back of a soda counter a sight right out of a Norma Rockwell painting. The enameled counter was clean and its half-dozen, round, red-leather stools in good repair. "Now let me see…one ginger ale…” She found a glass and used a tiny ice scoop to deposit a few cubes from under the counter before finding a can of ginger ale. The soda hissed and fizzed as it met the ice, bubbling up to the lip of the glass. Pushing a straw into the glass, she slid it across the counter.

Guen slid onto one of the stools, setting her purse on the stool adjacent.

“So you not meetin’ a man…”

“I am meeting someone, but not a beau.”

“He a local man? I knows just about everyone around here.”

“I’m not sure.”

“Well who then girl?” Eunice persisted. “I have ways of finding these things out but the gossipers might add details that just ain’t true.”

Guen paused, feeling a little self-conscious and suspecting who the town’s chief gossip was. She paused to turn attention to the glass of bubbling golden liquid set before her. Crossing herself she said grace over the beverage, and crossed herself again.

The old woman regarded her with amusement. “I ain’t never seen anyone pray over a ginger ale before…”

Guen regarded her congenially and shrugged. “I’m grateful for it and your hospitality.” She leaned over her drink and took a long sip for emphasis. The beverage was especially tasty after long hours of driving.

"Pious and beautiful. 'Dat's sweet. What they call you anyway?"

Guen had never heard it put that way before. "Oh? My name?"

"Yes-m…"

"Gigi—"

"Oh I knew'd a Genevieve back when I was growin' up."

"Oh. Sorry. Guenevere Grace…"

"Guenevere Grace? Oh. Well, that's pretty. Say, y'all want a free tarot reading? Somethin' to pass the time while you wait? It'll be on the house. Maybe I can find who out who y'all's meetin'?"

Guen detected a gleam in the old woman's eye, something that prickled the hair on the back of her neck. She shook her head, sending her blonde tresses bouncing around her face and shoulders. "It's nice of you to offer but no thank you."

She had been learning magic tricks—stage illusions, since she became her Uncle Henry's assistant at age ten. She set off as a magician in her own rite at sixteen. Stacking a deck was just a matter of practice and she was not falling for a sideshow parlor trick. The fortune salon had already made her especially wary.

"Well why not? It's just for fun…come on. One card…" A thick deck of over-sized cards appeared in the old woman's hands. She shuffled them with a dexterity that belied her age, pulled off the top card, and flipped it over.

Guen gasped at the sight. Her course on the occult included a class on tarot. She knew the card and slid off the stool, abandoning her drink and the invitation.

"Hold on cher, we ain't but started." Mrs. Bedlam called after her.

"It's fine. I'm fine, thank you."

"Come on now, don't be shy. Everyone wants the Lover Card and y'all got it right side up and everythin'."

"Mrs. Beldam—"

"Eunice, girl. We's becoming friends."

Guen looked around, desperate for a new topic of conversation. Her eyes settled on the steamboat memorabilia. She turned back to the elder. "I have some questions Mrs. Beldam—Eunice. What um…what can you tell me about the Belle?" She felt a sense of pride at her sudden inspiration.

"Ah…the Belle…" Setting the cards aside, Mrs. Beldam came out from behind the soda counter. "She's a fine boat, fine as they come. My kin and my Ernest's kin come up here on it all 'dem years ago. But times…" she paused to sigh and shake her head. "Times, they's a changin'."

Guen grimaced sympathetically at the woman's distress. "Did something happen?"

"County sold 'er to a big outfit outta Chicago. Word is, she ain't gonna be here no more."

They were interrupted by the creak and rattle of the outer screen door and the jingle of the bell over the inner door.

Footfalls announced the arrival of a tall, broad-shouldered Black man. His tailored black suit and polished black Oxfords silently announced his status. His eyes swept over the pair of women, lingering on Guen for an extra second. Guen did not hold it against him. She was accustomed to it. When they didn't look twice or linger a second she wondered if her hair was askew, her makeup off, or something else was wrong.

His second of interest completed, he fixed the elderly woman with a bright, cordial smile. "Hello Mrs. Beldam," he began, "How are you?"

"Well as I live and breathe, hello Mr. Fox. Y'all given any more thought to just leavin' be, sir?"

Fox shook his head and spoke to her in apologetic tones, "I'm afraid not, ma'am."

The corners of Mrs. Beldam's lips fell. "I'm all tore up to hear that."

Fox's expression became one of regret. "I'm sorry ma'am. As I've said before, it's just business."

"Yeah." Mrs. Beldam turned her gaze to Guenevere. "I gets the feelin' y'all are here to meet Guenevere Grace?"

"Indeed I am," He turned his attention to the younger woman and smiled broadly, "Miss Michaels, it is a pleasure…" Fox advanced upon the blonde, shaking her hand and exchanging professional pleasantries

"Ain't she pretty as a peach?" Mrs. Beldam smiled.

"Style, class, and brains, ma'am." He gestured, "Miss Michaels is a graduate of Princeton. She's quite a future ahead of her."

"Thank you, sir," Guen said, appreciating his tact.

"And wouldn't you say he's a fine lookin' man, girl?"

She blushed at the challenge. Fox had to be at least fifteen years older, likely more. "Yes. He is handsome, yes."

"And a fine dresser?"

"Yes." Guen nodded, feeling increasingly embarrassed.

"And a good voice."

"Yes…he does have a good voice."

"What about her, sir? She has beautiful legs and hips, the kind a man—"

"Ma'am."

"And those bosoms! I wish'd I still—"

"Ma'am…" Xavier fixed her with a stern look and held up a halting finger

"Alright I'll behave." Eunice conceded.

"Thank you," Xavier said.

Guen felt a sense of relief.

"As long as you don't!" She cackled.

"Oh my!" Brows raised, Guen glanced from Eunice back to Fox.

"Oh don't give me that look girl, I'm just getting' the field ready for plantin'."

Guen's great-grandmother had no filter either, but it was usually about someone's attitude or the quality of the food.

Izaak's grandma urged him to get her 'married up and makin' babies' but this was a professional relationship.

"Don't put the lady on the spot, like that Ma'am," Fox said. "She likes y'all but like most white women, she's too afraid to admit it, so we won't think bad of her."

Licking her lips, Guen spoke up. "I do like him." She spared Fox a glance, "And you're right. He is handsome and well dressed and well spoken, but our relationship is strictly professional."

Eunice frowned. "Shame, that."

"Well," Fox glanced around, "Before we go, let me get some souvenirs from you."

Mrs. Beldam's brows rose. "Well bless your heart. What would y'all like?"

Fox looked at the Belle display. "One of everything."

"I'll get you a big bag then." She turned to go to the back of the store.

Guen regarded him favorably. "This is so kind of you."

Johnson lowered his voice. "It's the least I can do. They don't like me around here all that much. That steamboat and this store are the only two points of interest in the county. If I can leave a more positive impression, then it's money well spent. "

"It can't be saved?"

"Boat's been operating in the red for three years, the county hasn't got the money, and the state and the Feds aren't stepping up. For what I bought it for, the county will have money for infrastructure and services—something they badly need around here."

Guen was about to pursue his reasoning when Mrs. Beldam returned with a large brown paper bag with handles and began to load it, by refolding t-shirts, and carefully placing fragile items among them. The elderly woman topped the small ensemble with an Belle hat.

"Here you are…" Fox produced a hundred dollar bill from a silver money clip. "No need for any change."

"Why thank you, sir." Beldam accepted the money.

"And for my ginger-ale," Guen fished a five-dollar bill from her purse and handed it over.

Eunice stroked the bills between her thumb and fingers. "Thank y'all, and have fun. I'm not sure what y'all are up to, but I'm sure y'all will look good together doin' it." She winked at Guen.

Guen felt the heat of a blush redden her cheeks. She struggled not to cringe and instead laughed affectedly. "Mrs. Beldam…" She gave the elderly woman a pleading look.

Fox spoke up. "Nothin' like that ma'am, it's just business."

"That what they be callin' it these days?" Eunice's eyes flashed with mischief.

Wearing an amused expression, Fox turned away, shepherding Guen towards the door with a gesture. "You take care, ma'am."

Guen turned one last time to express her thanks before allowing herself to be ushered through the door and outside.

"I'm sorry about that, sir…" Guen gave one last glance at the store's interior as they descended the stairs. "About what I said in there, what she kind-of made me—"

"Don't think anything of it. She wasn't wrong. I am a handsome, stylish, well-spoken man." He grinned before continuing. "You didn't do anything wrong, Miss Michaels. I get the feeling she's just living vicariously."

Guen's eyes went wide with exasperation. "I just wish she wasn't so lively about it! I mean…" She glanced back towards the store front.

Xavier chuckled and shook his head. "Forget about her I want to confirm a few things about you."

Suddenly cautious, Guen kept her expression pleasant. "What's that, sir?"

"I want to know…" he ducked his chin to one side and regarded her suspiciously, "If you're the same Guenevere Grace Michaels on the IMBD? The Scream Queen?"

"Oh…" Guen giggled with relief at the mention of the Internet Movie Database and gave him a tiny, playful curtsey of acknowledgement. "Yes…that's me."

"Is that what got you into this?"

"This—doing investigations…is partly what got me into movies."

"What was the other part, other than the obvious qualifications?"

"Thank you." She lowered her eyes demurely at the compliment. "Harry Houdini is a hero of mine. Not only his illusions and escape artistry but his quest to know about the afterlife. His magician training helped him discern frauds. He never found what he was looking for, but I can say I certainly have."

"So you're also a magician?"

"And escape artist as well, yes. It all dovetails together nicely for what I want to do," Guen explained.

"And what's that?" Fox set the paper bag on the hood of his SUV and leaned against its fender to regard her.

"Well, sir, I want to take all of my experiences and one day star in and produce my own paranormal documentary series."

"I admire your ambition, Miss Michaels," Fox smiled. "I think you'll realize your dream."

"Thank you sir!" She beamed both outwardly and inwardly, realizing she had just planted a seed—not the way Mrs. Beldam implied it, that way was for marriage, but maybe she had just found a deep pockets investor. She would have to play her cards right, but fortunately for her she was excellent at card tricks.

"Well…" He said, straightening up and opening the door of Guen's van, "I'll lead you over there." He held out his hand to assist her up and into the driver's seat.

Taking his hand she allowed him to help her up into her seat, entered sideways and kept her knees together before swinging her legs inward. She bit her bottom lip at the gallant gesture, it was unexpected but not unwelcome. "Follow me." He directed, and got into his Black Lexus SUV and pulled out of the parking lot. Guen in followed.

# # #

Smirking to herself, Eunice lurked between the aisles while watching the pair. "Girl gets any redder, she gonna explode—might just yet anyway." She cackled at the image. *She never has.* A voice hissed.
"What!" Eunice eyes went wide for a split-second before bursting into malicious cackles of delight. "Oh…dis gonna be sweet."
"He will be her serpent, and she, his Delilah…"
"I can't wait to see!" Eunice interlocked her fingers, raising her hands gleefully to her chest.
Once they were gone, and still cackling to herself, Eunice locked the front door, flicked off the lights, and hung up the 'closed' sign. Her feet left the ground and she floated to the fortune salon, pausing on the way to extract the lipstick-stained straw from Guen's glass.
A pungent mélange of scents wafted from the Fortune Room, smoldering sweet tobacco and cloying white rum mixed with the scents of dried fruits, roots, earth, herbs and

sulphur. To the uninitiated a sneeze was a common response. To her, it was an ambrosia for the nose.

The salon was a supply store for the initiated and a study, workshop, laboratory, and sanctum for Eunice. It was a place where she could ply her craft for gain, monetary and otherwise. It was a place where locals would come to her for charms, cures, curses, and divinations.

A leopard skin directly from Africa draped a purple velvet settee. Black velvet tapestries with voodoo vèvè sigils stitched in silver, gold, and brilliant purple. They hung between African folk masks. At the back of the room was an altar decorated with candles, gris-gris dolls, fresh flowers, a pewter bowl a chalice, a bottle of rum, a smoldering cigar and a grotesque winged statuette. She smiled at the statue as she took the pewter bowl, "We gonna have something sweet for you…"

Her throne-like wicker chair crackled as she sat down at a round table covered in a royal purple cloth. She lit a black candle and ignited a taper of incense. She set to work and tore the neat straight edges from the bills Guen and Xavier used to pay their bills. Once they were ragged, she dipped the tip of a goose quill into a pot of red ink. The nib scratched against the money's fabric as she traced symbols and the names Guen and Xavier. She dotted its edges with fragrant and acrid oils. Setting them aside, she lifted a small red glass jar onto the table and began to fill it with components of her spell: grains of rice, a spoonful of sugar, bits of orange peel, cinnamon and saffron, a spider web, a basil leaf, rose petals, and from a tiny sack no larger than her palm came powered pearl. After each component, she spoke an incantation, waving her hands over the red jar in an elaborate but precise manner. When the jar was nearly complete, she added the ragged money, inserted a red glass stopper, and shook it while chanting a final incantation. Completing the last note, her eyes narrowed, and she smiled. The stage was set. It was time to begin.

The previous night's rain and the totem she slipped into Fox's shopping bag, provided what she needed for her spell. Filling the pewter bowl, she chanted, and leaned forward to gaze into its surface. It shimmered before a clear picture of Xavier Fox's SUV took shape. Dipping the tip of her finger into the water, she swirled it around the edge of the bowl, faster and faster, only pausing to tap the water with the same finger, and begin anew.

"Yes! Yes!" She cackled, delighting in the results…

# # #

A thought struck Guen as she pulled onto the road leading into Blackwater. Maybe Mrs. Beldam's behavior was the result of her age. She felt a sudden pang of pity for her and regretted her reactions to the woman's antics. She decided she would add the elder to her nightly prayers.

As she followed Xavier towards town, the poverty she drove past disturbed her. Rundown houses signaled the beginnings of the town proper. Many of the homes nestled among the sassafras and sycamore trees were double-wide trailers. Rusted out cars set up on blocks decorated the lawns of some. The few people she saw sat on lawn chairs and sipped from bottles. They watched the two of them pass. A couple shot dirty looks and made obscene gestures in Xavier's direction.

She sighed to herself, trying to focus on the job and the radio's music but her mind kept going back to Eunice Beldam. The old woman's presumptions were disconcerting. She would never cheat on…on…Izaak! Eunice's goading was affecting her more than she thought. Mrs. Beldam was right about working with him. Xavier Fox was charming and handsome—and she did enjoy listening to his voice. Was he married? She didn't see a ring. Not that it mattered, they could still… An image of them together formed in her mind. Her skin warmed.

She gasped. Where did that thought come from! Of course it mattered. If he was married, his wife was certainly lucky. Flushed pink and breathing heavily, she struggled against the thoughts inundating and intruding upon her mind.

Guen rolled into a downtown that had seen better days. Most of the shops were boarded up. A trio of old men congregated on a bench outside the barbershop and pointed as Fox suddenly sped up, racing past the county's sheriff office.

Guen glanced from her speedometer to the black SUV and realized he had to be going at least twenty-miles-an-hour faster than the speed limit. A siren announced his sudden burst of speed had been detected as a white sheriff's car, its red and blue lights flashing, screeched out of the station's parking lot in pursuit.

Fox's SUV screeched nearly to a halt, only to speed up, then repeated the staggered halt, before speeding up again. After a block, the SUV and patrol car pulled into the town's only service station and garage where the short chase concluded.

Heart racing, Guen pulled her van over to the curb just short of the station. Face creased with worry, she leaned forward on the wheel vacillating between going to him and staying put. Eyes glassy, her breath caught as she watched the deputy at his window.

The minutes ticked by. She fidgeted in her seat, watching anxiously as Fox got out of his SUV and walked towards the garage. He looked back at her, smiled, and waved. Her heart soared.

The pair disappeared into the gas station's interior for several minutes before they came out again. The deputy got into his car and drove off and Guen got out, scurrying to meet Xavier. "Are you alright, sir? She reached to smooth his arm.

"Nothing to worry about, girl. My dinners cost more than a speeding fine in this state. Now come on, let's get to the boat. I'll drive."

It was reasonable offer after all, he knew the way. "Yes, sir." She handed him her key fob.

His hand found the small of her back. He directed her to the passenger side of the van. Opening the door for her, his hands found her waist and he lifted her onto the passenger seat. Her hands went to the hem of her skirt to tug it down. She stopped, hoping he would look, and giggled with elation when he did.

When Fox started the van, Al Green's Love and Happiness blasted out of the sound system. "You like Black music, girl?"

"Yes, sir, I love it."

Without hesitation, Fox began sang along with the tune, never missing a note. He looked over at her from time to time as he drove, giving her appreciative looks.

Her expression sultry, Guen's eyes never left him. The more she watched him, the more desirable he became. She watched his mouth, studied his strong hands on the wheel, and struggled not to touch her sides where he had touched her. She watched his gorgeous, liquid, deep brown eyes. The way he looked at her as he sang, sent shivers through her entire being.

The song's beat was a slow fever building to delirium. She brushed her hair from her neck, tilting her head away from him. Her chest rose and fell with heated breaths. She almost groaned when they arrived at the steamboat's mooring. Berthed on a slow moving tributary some miles from the Kentucky River, the Belle was a step back into the Victorian age. Five decks in height and longer than a football field, its opulent white gingerbread trim, bright red paddle wheels, and fluted black smoke stacks, made for an elegant contrast to the surrounding fecundity of the surrounding trees and river.

Amber party lights strung over the gate's small ticket shack clinked and bounced in the breeze. Power lines from the road stretched across the cracked asphalt of the parking lot to provide electricity.

Fox put the van in park and beamed at her, "What do you think?"

Guen's hand rose to her neck. "Thank you for the song. I've never had anyone sing to me before."

"I was inspired. What do you think of the Belle?"

"It looks nice." Guen said, not taking her eyes from Fox.

"You have any equipment you need carrying in?"

Guen shook her head to clear it. "Oh yes! Sorry, I'm so stupid!"

"In the back?"

"Yes. I'll just go back…" she unbuckled her seatbelt and pivoted out of her seat to squeeze between the front seats, casually gripping his shoulder to push herself past him.

Fox took her key fob and met her at the van's back doors. Opening it up, he found her slinging her messenger bag across her shoulder.

"Did you bring an overnight bag?"

She thrilled at his gaze, feeling butterflies in her stomach. Pulling the carryon luggage from its place among the props and chests of her magic act she handed it to him, and picked up a camera tripod.

"That's good. That's real good," he murmured, setting it down to lift her from the van down onto the asphalt.

"Thank-" The tripod slipped from her grasp, clattering to the ground.

Still clutching her waist, he drew her body to his. His lips pressed to hers.

Guen's eyes slid shut. She felt his soft lips pillowed against her own. Head swimming, she arched her body into his. Her knees felt weak, and her arms dangled limply at her sides.

For long seconds, Fox held her in his embrace before pulling back and smiling down at her. "I wanted to do that since the second I saw you."

She licked her lips, feeling her breath stolen, and her heart racing like it had only ever had with two men before. She gazed up at him, a shy smile curving her lips.

"You hear that?" He asked, still holding her waist.

Guen shook her head.

"The birds…and the frogs…" He cocked his head in emphasis at the chirping and croaking filling the air around them. "They're gettin' busy."

A high pitched giggle escaped her throat. She covered her mouth and blushed.

"Come on," he collected the suit case and tripod in one hand while taking her hand in the other. "I'll show you your room."

Fox eagerly led the way, ushering her across the gently swaying gangplank onto the Belle and up three flights of stairs. "This is it. The only new room on the boat." He thrust open the door pulled her inside, and dropped her luggage.

Guen followed. She kicked off her heels. Her messenger bag fell to the carpet with a thump, her purse hit the bed. Giggling, Guen launched herself into his arms, kissing him passionately. Her hands came to life, working feverishly, to push his jacket from his shoulders.

Fox loosened and tossed away his tie, returning the kiss, a hand in her hair and the other wrapped around her waist. "I want that tight, white, body." He snarled lustfully between kisses.

"Yes…" Guen hissed out the word, her entire being inflamed.

They fell onto the bed still kissing passionately. Fox's hand ran up her thigh and over her stocking-top, to grip her fair flesh.

Guen groaned, arching her back, feeling her bag digging into her back. "My purse…"

"You got something for me?"

"No…" She squirmed to find it. "It's jabbing me…" She paused to kiss him. Her hand found the bag, and tossed it across him to the floor.

As it flew, its flap opened, and spilled the contents onto them in a cascade of wallet, hair brush, lipstick, compact, mints, and rosary. The items struck them on their faces and heads.

Guen's eyes locked on her rosary and its St. Benedict medal and crucifix. Her eyes widened. "What am I doing?" She scrambled off the bed, looking at Fox with alarm.

"Guen? What's wrong?" Fox rolled off the bed, his expression puzzled.

"Stay back!" Guen's eyes flashed with fear.

"Hey…come back to bed, it'll be good. Real good." He held out his hand in a gesture of invitation.

Guen paused, surveying the scene, never letting Fox out of her sight. "What's happening to me? To us?"

"Girl, it's chemistry."

"No! No, it's not, this isn't me, I don't…" A thought struck her. "We've been cursed…enchanted…"

"What?" Fox regarded her incredulously. "Come on girl, you were—"

"No. It wasn't me, it was her."

"Who?"

"Mrs. Beldam. She did something, some sort of incantation, a love charm."

"Girl…" Fox grimaced, "That's just silly. Now come on…" He took a step for her, his expression, consoling.

Heart racing, Guen's posture became rigid. She stabbed a finger at her bag. "Hand me my purse."

"What?"

"Now."

"All right…all right, it's all good." Fox stooped down to retrieve it and offer it to her.

Guen snatched the bag from him and opened the flap. Janet had guns, Izaak his interposing size and strength, she had her own resources, pepper spray was one of them but she sought something else. In its own sheath, next to the pepper spray was a tiny bottle of holy water. Unstoppering it, she flung droplets at him, vertically and horizontally to mimic the shape of a cross. "Vade retro me Satana—Vadre Retro."

"What!" Fox protested as the water droplets flew through the air. He flinched and blinked hard…once…then twice. "What…" he looked at Guen sideways. "What just happened?"

"Mrs. Bedlam…I think she enchanted us, cursed us. It's a kind of obsession."

"Oh come on…" Fox regarded her skeptically.

"Did you notice her fortune telling salon?"

"Yeah, but—"

"She wanted to hurt us—you specifically with me as the weapon."

Fox frowned at her.

"I don't do this, Mr. Fox. This kind of casual…it isn't me. I have had the same boyfriend for four years, I hope to marry him. I don't ever cheat-ever."

"Okay, that's all good, but a weapon?"

"Yes. First we would…" she gave the bed an anxious glance. "Then I would…" she paused for a split-second to find the right word, "…object. Which would bring in the courts…and you wouldn't be able to take the Belle away."

"Goddamn that's cold!"

Guen resisted the urge to frown at the blasphemy.

Fox turned away from Guen, his face twisted into a furious scowl. "What a bitch. What a stone cold bitch."

Guen grimaced sympathetically. "She's in a terrible place."

"That woman needs to be in a terrible place-worse than here."

"If she continues, she will be," Guen said softly.

"Okay…okay." Fox's shoulders sank, his scowl faded. "I believe you and I'm sorry." He regarded Guen with concern. "Did I hurt you?"

Guen pressed her lips together, halfway to tears over what might have happened. "No. No, you didn't. But we have things to do."

"What things?"

Guen straightened her clothing, and knelt down to retrieve her messenger bag. She unbuckled its straps to draw forth a small black binder. Guen flipped through the laminated and tabbed pages. "First you're going to pray this." She held the binder up and open to him.

"Pray? I haven't been to church in years."

"I suggest you start but in the meantime, do you own this boat?"

"Yeah." He nodded his expression still skeptical about the pro-offered binder.

"Then you can protect it from curses and infestations, and her sending reinforcements." She caught his expression, and offered it emphatically, pushing it towards his hands. "Just read the words aloud, and believe. That's important, you must have faith."

"I'm not even Catholic."

"He'll hear you."

She watched and listened as Fox gripped the binder, sometimes stumbling over the phrasing of the perimeter prayer.

"…Amen. Okay." Fox offered it back to her.

"Just one, I'll go first if you don't mind. I want to guard against retaliation. If she figures out that we're out from under her spell, she might send reinforcements to attack us or the people we love."

"She can do that?"

Guen regarded him patiently. "Sir, you hired me because you believe there are ghosts on your steamboat. This shouldn't be too much of a stretch."

Guen finished the prayer, and waited for Fox to likewise complete it before replacing the binder in her bag. "That should take care of any spies sent to watch us."

"Spies?"

"Minions. No…that isn't correct. She thinks they work for her, but really she's just a means to an end."

"What end?"

"To lead as many astray as possible, but we should be fine now."

"Alright Ms. Michaels. You're the expert and if you want to go, I'll understand—and I'm sorry."

"I understand too. That neither of us were acting as ourselves, but now we are. You did nothing wrong and neither did I. So there is nothing to be sorry for."

"So?"

"So I will do what you hired me to do. I suggest you not be alone on the boat and take accommodations in Lexington while the work goes on here."

"Princeton definitely picked the right student." He smiled cordially.

"Thank you. Now, once I clean up the contents of my purse, we can get started on sending these ghosts on to heaven."

"Heaven?

"Ghosts are souls trapped in purgatory, asking for help to be released. If I—if we can help them along, your hauntings will be over."

"Sounds good to me." He crouched down to pick the contents of her purse from the floor and set them on the bed for her to replace in her purse.

# # #

They began in the engine room. The enormous steam engine that once drove the boat's paddle wheels was in the process of being removed. Tools and work lamps lay strewn about the floor, a testament to the sudden departure of the workmen frightened from the place by the ghostly appearance of the long deceased stoker. Setting up her tripod and camera, Guen's attempts to coax a manifestation netted a cold draft. Offering him reassurances, followed by requiem prayers, the cold dissipated. An impressed Xavier moved them along to the paddle house on the starboard side.

Young Andy Stockton lost his life after a night of heavy drinking in the Belle's saloon. He fell over the railing and into the Belle's starboard paddle wheel to be dragged under and drowned. His ghost could occasionally be seen in the early morning hours repeating his fate. Setting up her equipment again, Guen called to him by name. The spike on her electronic field meter indicated something more just the two of them was present. Guen reassured him he was not forgotten, and his family was waiting to see him. She said the requiem prayer to move him along. Just as before a sudden cold manifested and dissipated.

They moved on to the saloon. Opulent with its mahogany wainscoting, brass fittings, and Tiffany glass, Guen was pleased to learn Fox had no plans to alter its historical beauty. Setting up, Guen took a seat at the round table where Archibald Fowler was murdered.

When she called to him he appeared, transparent and still dressed in the finery of a top hat and suit. He smiled briefly as Guen explained, how Fowler's killer had been judged and that he no longer needed to stay. Justice had been served. She completed their interaction with the opening of the funeral requiem, chanting it in Latin, as Fowler vanished into the ether.

Standing up, Guen turned to see a wide-eyed Xavier, a few steps further back than where he started. She regarded him sympathetically. "How are you doing, sir?"

"That was…"

"A ghost, one that has moved on from your boat."

"You're sure now?" He looked past her at the chair where the ghost appeared, "I don't need him showing up and scaring off the workers again."

"I never have repeat customers, sir." She moved to her tripod to remove her phone. "Thank you for allowing me to record."

"Well I figured if you choose to include the Belle—in spite of what happened, it might drum up some business for me. Speaking of which, I've been thinking...about our bookings. You'd make a great opening act on our first cruise."

Guen recognized the conciliatory gesture. Given their interactions less than two hours before she was still cautious but kept her feelings from her face. "I'm flattered sir, I don't normally handle those negotiations anymore, my agent does." She produced a card. "He'll talk to your booking agent."

"Let me take you to dinner in Lexington—it's the least I can do," he said, accepting the card.

"I was—"

The lights flickered. A deafening crash of thunder left their ears ringing. The boat lurched sideways. The camera tripod clattered to the floor and slid sideways. Still in heels, Guen began to stumble. Fox reached out with a steadying arm to catch her. The skies opened and a deluge of rain began to fall, battering the Belle's top deck. A hurricane wind whipped and howled around the boat, rocking it side to side, slamming it against the dock.

"What the hell!" Fox shouted over the cacophony. Hunched into a half crouch his arm surrounded Guen's waist, steadying her as the boat surged.

Guen's heart froze in realization. "That's where it's from...hell!" Her eyes darted about, heart racing, utterly bewildered.

The ship's lights went out, emergency lights over exit doors flicked on automatically.

"Mrs. Beldam!" Fox asked his eyes wide.

"Yes!" Guen shouted, gripping his encircling arm. "I need my bag!"

The low light of the emergency lamps did little to illuminate the darkened corner of the saloon.

"I see it!" Fox shouted over the rain and continuous crashes of thunder.

Guen followed his gaze. The bag had slid across the floor and under a table. Still in his embrace, the two of them wobbled towards the table. Bolted to the floor, it remained in place but its chairs, and all the others in the saloon were on their sides and sliding to and fro, their rumbling and scratching adding to the overhead clamor.

Dropping to her knees, Guen began to crawl beneath the table, reaching to grab its center spindle to avoid joining the wayward furnishings.

"I got you!" Fox gripped the edge of the table with one hand while gripping her hip with the other. Whenever a piece of furniture slide in their direction, Fox would send out a foot to intercept and redirect it.

Panting with fear, Guen flipped open the flap of her bag, feeling around for a flashlight, finding one, she flicked it on inside the bag, for what she truly sought.

"My binder…" She turned and shouted to Fox, "where is it!"

Fox thought for a second. "I left it with you purse and luggage in the stateroom!"

"We have to get it!"

"Come on!" Fox helped her from beneath the table, and lifted her over his shoulder.

"What are you doing!" Guen protested arching her back and squirming to try and see his face.

Gripping the edge of the table with one hand and wrapping his other arm around her legs, Fox stood. "I'm going to carry you up!"

"No!"

"Yes! It will be faster!" Timing his steps to the lurching of the boat, Fox went from table to table, aiming for the staircase outside the saloon's main entrance.

Guen's heart was in her throat, she took the heavy black flashlight from her bag and aimed it at the floor to guide his steps as he dodged errant furniture and struggled from hand hold to hand hold.

Reaching the stairs, Fox grunted, pausing several times, holding the railing in a white-knuckle grip to keep from falling.

Guen had visions of them both falling and being too hurt to stand. She began to pray Hail Mary's over and over again, not stopping even when Fox set her down on the upper deck.

Gripping the flashlight between them, they held onto each other, bouncing off the walls of the passage, moving with determination towards the stern and her room.

Inside, Guen's light pierced the darkness. The doors of the empty wardrobe were open and swinging. Fox tossed the only piece of movable furniture, the stateroom's desk chair, into the bathroom. The pelting rain and the accompanying unnatural darkness made seeing out the window all but impossible.

Guen's eyes fell upon the binder, it, along with her suitcase were on the floor and sliding across the carpet. The swaying of the boat slammed the door shut with a definite click. Gripping the room's vanity for support, Fox watched her pick up the binder and began to flip through it. "I thought that perimeter prayer was supposed to stop this!"

"A hundred yards isn't far enough to stop a storm!" she shouted, frantically flipping through the pages. Still on her knees, she began to pray the deliverance prayer, shouting it at the top of lungs.

Repeating the prayer a third time, the wind began to abate, the rain turned from a downpour to a spring shower, the thunder stopped.

Panting, her throat sore, Guen rose from the floor and slumped onto the edge of the bed.

"You did a miracle, an honest to God miracle."

"I did nothing. I asked for help, and we got it."

Fox tentatively sat down on the bed, an arm's length from her. "I think I'm going to start going back to church."
"That's a good—"
BAM! The state room's door shuddered.
Guen's heart jumped into her throat. She starred at the door.
"What the hell!" Fox stood up, also starring at the door.
BAM! The door's surface showed a crack.
BAM! The state room's thin door shuddered, and then came apart.
Guen screamed retreating back towards Fox who squared his body to confront the threat.
The stench of ammonia, rotting eggs and decomposing cabbage wrinkled their nostrils. A tall brutish figure shuffled into the state room. African by ethnicity but wrinkled and gray, it wore the remnants of a muddy black suit. Gums and teeth blackened and eyes milky white, it advanced fearlessly, swinging its fists like clubs.
"Look out!" Guen screamed a warning.
"Come on you ugly, son-of-a-bitch!" Fox advanced aiming a well placed kick to the intruder's abdomen sending it back towards the door.
Starring in horror, Guen stood. Her mind racing as to what it could be. A zombie? Had Eunice Beldam animated a corpse?
Undeterred, the zombie advanced, still swinging its fists and gnashing its blackened teeth.

Fox met it in the center of the small room, straining against its strength. He grunted when one of the zombies massive fists struck his head. Dazed he struggled to remain standing, and retreated a step. A second fist sent him to the floor.

"Xavier!" Guen screamed, eyeing the zombie while trying to put as much space between her and it.

The zombie advanced, sopping wet and stinking of hell. It reached to grab her.

Guen ducked beneath its marauding hands, scampering up onto the bed and down its length. She couldn't stop it. She needed to get to safety and get to help. The sheriff's station was only ten minutes away.

Still clutching the flashlight, Guen reached the passage, and turned towards the stern and the nearest stairwell. Her light fell upon Eunice Beldam, floating six inches off the deck and clutching a pale pink gris gris doll with yellow yarn for hair.

She turned to run the other way as the zombie emerged from the room blocking the passage.

Eunice held up the doll and a hat pin. Grinning, she jabbed the pin deep into the doll's back.

Guen had never known such terrible pain. Body arching she screeched and collapsed to the floor unconscious.

Eunice floated forward, the doll still clutched in her wrinkled hands. She paused, over Guen's inert form. "Why did y'all have to get all holy and sanctimonious? I was enjoying the show. But no matter…you'll serve…you'll serve…"

She turned her attention to the zombie. "Ernest you pick that man up in there, nice and high, high as y'all can."

The zombie returned the room. He lifted Fox to his chest, then over his head until Fox's body touched the ceiling. Taking Guen's flashlight, Eunice flooded the compartment with light. Watching her minion she pointed to the floor. "Now drop 'em."

Fox fell the eight feet to the floor with a heavy thump.

"Now do it again." Eunice ordered.

The zombie complied without a sound, repeating the action, once more, and one more again.

"That outta do it." Eunice nodded and turned to crouch down next to Guen. "This one is a little stringy in places." She pinched Guen's upper arm, "But there's enough…"

She prodded the side of the blonde's breast and reached an intruding hand under her skirt to test her thigh and rump. "Pick it up, the feast of renewal has dun' come early."

Reaching down, the zombie picked Guen up, to cradle her in its arms and follow its mistress into the night.

# # #

Eunice Beldam smirked at the tied and collapsed girl folded into a ball inside the gibbet. Scarcely shoulder-width, the tiny iron cage had held many meals over the years. This one had never been touched. She would be especially tasty for her and her master.

Cold burrowed through Guen's senseless state. She shivered and her skin goose-pimpled. Her eyes fluttered open to bars, iron bars, all around her. She was on the floor, her clothes had been taken. Her arms and wrists were numb and tucked behind her. She quickly realized she was bound. The realization brought her knees to her chest. Her head on a swivel, she began to examine the one room stone cottage.

Eunice turned from a plank kitchen-counter to peer through the cage's bars. "Ah there she is…our tasty morsel…"

"Let me go." Guen's response was both part request and part demand.

"What would we have for dinner then?" She lifted a clever from a butcher's block and cackled uproariously at Guen's frightened gasp before turning back to her preparations. Trembling, and keeping her knees and shins before her, Guen examined her surroundings. The cramped cage was tall enough for her to stand, but was only a little wider than her shoulders. Its lock, built into the bars, was vintage, something out of the nineteen century.

The cottage's exposed beams were festooned with dusty spider-webs. Its tiny windows were dusty and darkened by the night.

Looking to her left, she startled at the sight of a hideous altar. Her eyes darted from object to object. Her breaths came in soft, horrified sobs. A dozen outward facing skulls ringed its perimeter, a single, black candle protruded from the top of each. The candles' glow illuminated hideous symbols of darkness: a dagger, a cup, a great tome bound with skin, and a statue of a humanoid goat sitting cross legged on an inverted pentagram. Aghast, Guen averted her gaze to examine the remainder of the cottage.

The contents of a cauldron popped and steamed over a fire in the hearth. The scent of hot oil competed with the scent of wood smoke. Above it, on the mantle, a pink gris gris doll, with its yellow yarn hair, she recognized the crude version of herself. Next to the cage was a table set with a lacy table cloth and cambric napkins, fine bone china, and what appeared to be antique silverware.

Across the room, her clothes and shoes were piled next to a double bed covered with a patchwork quilt. She shivered at the image of the woman touching her. The kitchen consisted of a counter constructed of planks, a wash basin, and shelves containing some modern canned goods mixed with glass bottles, and clay and glass jars. Eunice seemed to be chopping something at the counter. Above the old woman, hung a pair of shackles, spaced too far apart for her arms to reach… She cringed. Beneath the counter a smaller iron cauldron rested, exactly at the midpoint between the manacles. Guen began to sweat, and shivered again.

Eunice reached for a clay crock from the shelf and opened it and began an expletive-laden tirade, seemingly directed at herself that ended with an admission. "Only one thing to do, go get more…"

Holding the tiny clay pot, Eunice floated across the floor, pausing to regard her captive with eyes like oily black pearls. Her voice came out as a guttural, lisping rasp, "You have plagued us long enough. How delicious you will be."

Guen reflexively tried to cross herself, her bonds bit into her flesh, keeping her from the sacramental gesture. She emitted a soft whine, her brow furrowing with fear.

The guffaw that came back was not Eunice's cracked cackled but that of a guttural male voice.

Through trembling lips, Guen offered a tremulous rebuttal, one she prayed many times before, St. Michael's prayer in the official language of the church, Latin. "Santce Michael Archangele, defende nos in proelio, contra nequitiam et insidias diaboli esto praesidium. Imperet illi Deus, supplices deprecamur: tuque, Princeps militiae caelestis, Satanam aliosque spiritus malignos, qui ad perditionem animarum pervagantur in mundo, divina virtute, in infernum detrude. Amen." She glowered at the thing before her.

Eunice snarled like a beast from the pit. Nostrils flaring, she advanced on the cage, ringing her hands against the bars.

They shuttered with the impact. "We will silence you yet, sow!"

Guen retreated against the bars, their cold, hard surfaces digging into her back. She realized Eunice Beldam was beyond possessed, she was completely subjugated, a willing subject.

The voice coming through Eunice guffawed and proclaimed, "He's not coming to save you."

Lies. Guen thought instinctively.

The blackened eyes vanished with a blink. Eunice looked at her, her face pinching with mirth. "Y'all just be patient, girl. Dinner won't be long comin'." She went to the door and bellowed, "Ernest! Y'all get in here, now!"

Guen's nostrils wrinkled at the sudden putrescence filling the cottage's air. She recoiled, watching the door as the now familiar figure shuffled through. By the light of the cottage's single light bulb, she could see the tall, Black, zombie. He was hideous to behold, rotting, wrinkled, gray, and milk-eyed. She half-turned her face to keep him in her peripheral vision.

"Ernest here, will keep y'all company whiles I gets the last ingredient." She held up a sharp, wooden handled paring knife and pointed it at Ernest. "Y'all keep an eye on her." She floated through the open door, slamming it tight behind her.

Still trembling from the exchange, Guen surreptitiously looked at the zombie. He stood stark still, like a statue, unfocused on her or seemingly anything at all.

Her stomach turned at the stench. She was glad her last meal was hours ago and wondered how long she had been there, and about poor Xavier. She had to get out, even if it meant dodging around the zombie and running naked into the night for help. She wasn't even sure where she was, but heard the hum of a small outboard boat motor start, and begin to fade. Was she on an island? Would she have to swim? Were there alligators this far north? She was sure there were snakes, poisonous ones. She silently prayed for help and began her escape.

Flexing and un-flexing her hands, she grunted against the pain. Her bonds were too snug to loosen. What she did next would be excruciating to the point of impossible for most. Guen had been stretching the ligaments in her limbs and fingers for years, making it possible to escape handcuffs, manacles, and strait jackets. Pressing her lips together in concentration, she used her right thumb to push against the joint of her opposite thumb, quickly dislocating it. With a bit of tugging, her hand slipped free. Using her freed hand, she manipulated her thumb back into place. She attempted to bring both hands around front to pull the other bond free and found the leather strap above her elbows kept her hands at her flanks. Her hands could not reach each other.

Standing, she began to reach and wriggle for the bond at her elbow. She flicked it repeatedly, until it slid down over her elbow. She repeated the gesture until both elbows were cleared and the thin cord fell to her feet.

Despite all of her activity, Ernest never stirred.

Crouching down, Guen examined the lock. If she had her locksmith tools, the old lock would be something she could have easily picked when she was twelve.

She regarded the table, pondering the silverware. The bars were tightly spaced. Dislocating her right thumb again, she slid her hand between the bars, stretching for the fork that rested beside the plate.

"Come on" She groaned in frustration, perspiration forming on her brow. Grunting, she stretched and strained, attempting to force her arm through the gap, but it was too thin for her elbow.

Panting with exertion, she set upon a new tactic. She could not reach the utensils but she could reach the table cloth. Reaching again, she pinched the black fabric, carefully tugging it closer and closer to the edge of the table, the utensils clinking against the plate and each other. She watched in horror, crying out in anguish, as the goblet toppled over sending the plate, and utensils crashing to the floor. The knife landed near the base of her cage. Her hand shot out to grab it.

She jerked her head around to regard the zombie. He remained statue like, completely uninterested in her actions.

Biting her lip, she slipped the knife into the lock, after several moments of stirring it around in search of the tumbler to release the lock, she realized it would not work. It needed to be shaped like a 'J' to do what she needed to do.

She needed to bend it. Strong as her fingers were from years of coin and card tricks, the silverware's tensile strength was too much. She needed a vice, or…as a thought struck her, an improvised vice. Slipping the knife under the edge of the cage, she grunted, lifting it up, slowly, gently, until it was bent at nearly ninety-degrees. Inserting the improvised pick into the lock, she tried again. The locked clicked open in an instant. She was free.

Heart pounding, she regarded the zombie. She was faster and more agile than him but if he struck her or grabbed her, it would be over. She could not leave without the gris gris doll or her clothes, Eunice could make use of even the smallest swatch of her clothing to evoke hardship for her. If she could, she would burn the place to the ground but the doll was extremely important. She had to take it with her. It had to blessed by a priest, destroyed, and the pieces or ashes cast into running water, a river or a lake to render it impotent.

Equally important, she could not touch it with her hands. Anyone who did not share Eunice's allegiance would suffer a debilitating curse. She needed a way to move it and carry it. There was a basket of vegetables on the counter that she could use, and there was an iron fire poker sticking out of the wood box next to the hearth.

It all came down to the zombie.

Could she move across the room, dump the vegetables, sweep the doll into the basket, retrieve her clothes and get out the door before he got her?

The drone of the returning outboard motor quickened her pulse. There was no time left. Guen burst from the cage, making for the counter. Ernest stirred to life in pursuit, shuffling after her, his hands and arms outstretched. Guen evaded his clutches, by circling around behind him. She dumped the vegetables onto the floor and seized the poker. Atop the mantle, besides her doll, there was another, dark brown with black yarn for hair, the red shaker jar, and various other bric-a-brac. Ducking beneath the zombie's swiping hands, she used the poker to sweep all of it into the basket.

The zombie halted.

The door opened with a squeal.

Eunice Bedlam floated in, her knife in one hand and a bunch of dead nettle in the other. "What! How did y'all get out? Ernest, grab her!"

The zombie stood still.

Guen held the poker up defensively, and wondered if she could grab one of the cleavers or butcher knives from the counter.

"Ernest grab her!" Eunice screeched.

The zombie remained motionless.

"What…what have y'all done, girl?" Her head wove back and forth like a cobra's. Her eyes came to rest on the mantle. "Where…y'all gonna give me back my things, just this instant!"

"Stay back!" Guen raised the poker, preparing to swing it with all her might.

"You gimme that back, now!" Eunice demanded.

Guen spared the basket a glance, among the items swept into the basket was a leather sheath, tied with black ribbon, a phylactery. What was inside the sheath contained Ernest's soul, whoever controlled it, controlled him.

"No." Guen stated firmly. She knew in the back of her mind that what she was about to do was going to require penance. Guen pointed at Eunice. "Ernest…put her in the cage."

The zombie turned away from Guen, lumbering towards his former mistress.

"Ernest! No! I am your wife. Y'all will listen—" Eunice screeched, retreating out the door with the zombie in pursuit.

Guen glanced from the door to her pile of clothing, she needed to get dressed, just her blouse and skirt would do, the rest she could pile into the basket. Bending down to her belongings she found them cut to shreds, Eunice had cut her clothing from her. Everything but her shoes was sliced and torn. Casting about, she considered the chest of

Eunice's clothes, or the patch-work quilt from the bed, the quilt won out.

Wrapping it around her shoulders, Guen headed for the door, and felt a profound sense of relief at the sound of approaching sirens. Leaving the cottage, she saw the red and blue flashing lights of sheriff's cars, their headlights illuminating the narrow spit of land stretching out towards the cottage.

Wrapping the quilt around her like a bath towel, and pondering the entity's threat, she strode to meet them.

# # #

After his assault, Xavier stirred from his unconsciousness to make a groggy 911 call before falling unconscious again. A life flight brought him to the trauma center in Lexington where Guen spent much of the following morning in the quiet solitude of the hospitals chapel with detectives from the Kentucky Department of Criminal Investigation and agents from the Federal Bureau of Investigation.

After interviewing her, the agents shocked her with a few details of their investigation. Eunice Beldam was one hundred and sixteen years old. Guen nearly fell out of her chair when they revealed over the past fifty years, twelve young women had gone missing in and around Black Water. They were sending the skulls in Eunice's cottage for forensic analysis to determine if the belonged to any of the missing women. Finally, to Guen's relief, Eunice's body was found next to a badly decomposed corpse two miles from her cottage. They assured Guen that she was no longer in danger.

She did not share their optimism. The encounter with the entity in the cottage left her feeling wary. Sitting in the chapel after the agents left, she gazed at its stained glass window of Christ in the Garden of Gethsemane and wondered if He put her into these situations to foil His enemy.

She sat on the edge of Xavier Fox's bed, gently holding his bandaged hand and quietly praying. A squeeze signaled his wakefulness.

Fox smiled at her through swollen lips. "A sight for sore everything."

Guen's shoulders sagged with relief. "I'm so glad you're all right, sir. I'm sorry I—"

"Nothing for you…" Fox licked his lips. "Nothing for you to be sorry for Miss Michaels. I'm glad you're safe."

"We got them, sir. Eunice and Ernest, we got them."

"That will make renovations easier." He smiled as his eyes began to slip shut.

"I'll let you rest, sir."

"Love and happiness, Miss Michaels." His voice began to drift off.

"And may God bless you, sir."

What Lies Beneath

The high-pitched chatter of cicadas greeted them as Guenevere Grace Michaels, eased the black van through the tunnel of green fecundity. A bed of weeds covered the gravel crunching and crackling under the van's tires. The branches of encroaching trees swished and thumped against its sides.

"My grandma drives faster than this on a Sunday afternoon." Janet Yamashita, her best friend, roommate, and business partner, grumbled from the passenger seat. She rested her feet stockinged feet on the dashboard.

Guenevere spared her a glance. "Your grandmother lives up in the mountains—*in Japan!*"

"And she drives faster than this."

"I'm not scratching up the van to get there thirty seconds faster."

"You'd never make it as a pizza delivery driver." Janet looked back down at her mobile.

"Luckily, I have a day job."

Janet glanced up when a branch smacked her window. "She didn't say we would have to drive through a jungle to get to this place."

"I like it. It's quiet, and cool, and pretty." Guenevere gestured to the foliage, as the sun pierced through the green canopy.

"And there's probably bears." Janet scoffed.

Struck by the thought the blonde considered it, "Maybe…" A second thought overran the first. "You brought your gun didn't you?"

"I always bring my gun."

Guenevere fixed her with a look of reproach. "She's a real estate agent, not to a mob boss."

"Two teenagers went missing at this house, you know." Janet warned.

"That was decades ago and it was in the woods, not *at* the house."

"And a hunter."

"Ten years ago."

Sighing, Janet lifted her feet from the dash to fish her grandfather's police revolver out of her purse and transfer it and its holster into one of their equipment bags.

Guenevere glanced over at her friend. "I think this one could be a good one for the series."

"You think they're all good for the series."

"Come on…" Guenevere tilted her head plaintively. "A classic haunted house story? What's better than that?"

"If there are any ghosts," Janet said skeptically.

"Well, from the information that Cheryl sent us…the thought of those poor little kids freezing to death in the nursery—and that family in the 1920s. They spent all that money refurbishing the house and only stayed one night. If that doesn't scream haunted I don't…"

Janet sat up as they rounded a bend and the Monahan house came into view. "Well, we're here. So I guess we'll find out."

Set in a clearing, the Victorian home's slat-board exterior was haggard and gray. Its white paint peeled from years of weathering. The windows on every floor were shuttered and boarded over. At the end of the lane sat an old carriage house that seemed ready to fall in on itself. Parked beside it was a burgundy mini-van. Its owner, a woman in a tan skirt suit, stood on the sidewalk, its cement slabs sunk into the turf, forming a gray archipelago. She looked up and gave a friendly wave as Guenevere rolled the van to a stop.

"Looks like we got here in time for the annual lawn mowing." Janet sniffed at the windrowed lawn. It looked like a hay mower was used to cut the thigh-high grass down to ankle-high spikes of green and brown.

"Well maybe once we give it the all clear, someone will buy it and you can come mow it weekly. Hand me my shoes, please."

"Hah! Come back here?" Janet turned to find Guenevere's crimson pumps from behind her seat.

Guenevere accepted the shoes with thanks and changed from her flats. "Everything okay?" she drew back her lips for signs of lipstick on her teeth. The blonde wore a blouse to match her shoes, a fitted black mini-skirt, and suntan hose.

Janet took a quick look. "Beautiful. Now, how do I look?"

Guenevere looked over her friend. She wore a white silk blouse tied at the neck with a slender bow, a flared black mini-skirt, black tights, and black pumps. "Polished and professional…perfect."

Only two years out of college, the blouses and skirts, hosiery and heels were the pair's attempt to project a level of maturity and professionalism.

"I'm ready." Janet held up a camcorder.

"And…3…2…1… It's Wednesday, September fifteenth, we're at the site of the Monahan house, eight miles from Gilboa, New York, the site of a reported haunting…and…cut.

"Got it"

"How's it look?" Guenevere asked.

"It's just an intro."

"And?"

"The lighting is fine, you look fine."

"Thank you. Okay, lets' go" Guen seized the messenger bag that served as a purse, attaché case and mini-ghost hunting kit. She led the way towards their client, Cheryl Hicks.

In her early thirties, Hicks wore her sandy-blonde hair in a bob. She removed a pair of gardening gloves to shake their hands. "I hope you didn't have any trouble finding the place."

Guenevere glanced at Janet. "I have an expert navigator."

"Oh good," Cheryl led the way towards the house. "I Googled you, I didn't know you were a movie star too."

"Thank you. It was just the three, I've moved on to other things." Guenevere replied.

"But you won an award? A Scream-Queen?"

"She's done other things too, some TV shows, commercials, modeling." Janet added.

"And Janet is my assistant for our stage magic shows." Guenevere smiled at her friend, grateful for the rescue.

"So you're a magician too?"

"Top Hat Magic and Illusions," Janet supplied at card from her purse.

"And you also hunt ghosts?" The realtor delved into her purse for a ring of brass keys.

"Ever since I was twelve, yes." Guen nodded.

Cheryl's eyebrows rose."Twelve? I'm be too scared to do that now!"

Guenevere laughed. "Most of the time it's just sitting in the dark looking at computer screens."

"And you as well?" Cheryl looked at Janet.

"No, she kind-of dared me into it in college."

"Six years ago," Guenevere supplied.

"Sounds like I picked an experienced team!" Cheryl enthused. "Let's go inside and get out of the sun."

Cheryl led the way up the steps and onto the porch, despite its recent sweeping, the remaining flecks of paint gave it a worn out look.

"It might not look like much, but it's almost two hundred years old. It has good bones, all oak construction. It was a station on the Underground Railroad. That's another reason to save it." The realtor stomped the heel of her foot on the porch for emphasis. "We've been trying to sell this home since my grandfather went into the reality business seventy years ago but the house's reputation hasn't exactly had them pounding down our doors to buy it. Hopefully with your help, we can get a family in here and get it off the books." She beamed at them and produced a shiny brass key to thrust into the newest part of the entire house, the front door's deadbolt lock.

"Wait…" Janet halted, looking up at the porch ceiling. A butterfly was ensnared in a spider web.

The two blondes watched as Janet reached up on tip toes, to sever the web's strands and deftly catch the butterfly.

"Is it alive?" Cheryl asked, watching Janet carefully pluck the bits of silk from the insect's delicate wings.

"Yes." Janet smiled triumphantly, as it fluttered away. "You have to be careful not to damage their wings."

"That was nice of you." Cheryl smiled.

Janet returned the smile with a shrug, and accepted a proffered tissue from Guenevere to wipe the web from her fingers.

Cheryl turned back to the door, glancing over her shoulder as she talked. "It's good you're not afraid of spiders because there's no shortage of them around here."

"We've been in more than a few places that had their share." Guenevere said.

"I'm sorry to say you've found another one." Cheryl grimaced and pushed the front door inward.

The door protested their intrusion with a long squeal that set their teeth on edge. Musty, stale air assailed their nostrils. "Sorry about that." Cheryl cringed and fixed them with an apologetic look. "One of the things to fix once you declare the house ghost-free."

The realtor directed their attention to a pair of corn brooms just inside the door. "You'll need those to clear the way into some of the rooms. Just let me go into the pantry and flip on the power." She produced a flashlight from her purse, grabbed one of the brooms, and strode down the hall, swiping it up and down before her to clear cobwebs.

The pair exchanged glances, shrugged good-naturedly, and examined their surroundings. The entry rug, though barely used, was fading and moth-holed. The varnish of the hardwood floor peeled throughout. The white paint on the walls was chipped and flaking. The balustrade was covered by a diaphanous silk net of spider-webs.

"Definitely has that not-lived-in look." Janet observed.

Guenevere lifted a finger to her lip in a shushing gesture and shook her head.

"I know." Janet rolled her eyes.

Guenevere took a few steps and examined the place further. To their left, dusty white sheets shrouded the parlor furnishings. To their right a web covered chandelier tented out to an equally dusty dining room table. It fastened itself to the high-backed dining chairs. "Definitely not lived-in…" she murmured to herself.

There was a metallic clang from the back of the house, followed by a muffled expression of frustration. Cheryl's footfalls signaled her return. She sighed, fixing them with an apologetic look. "I'm sorry, ladies. It doesn't look like we have lights. The utilities company was supposed to have that done. I'll understand if you want to come back. We'll compensate you for your time and mileage."

Guenevere shook her head in refusal. "It's okay. Most of the places we visit don't have lights, but we have lots of them. I have three in my bag." She patted it for emphasis.

"Plus the generator in the van," Janet added.

Cheryl's brows rose. "Wow! You come prepared."

"One black out in a haunted asylum is all it takes." Guenevere giggled in memory.

"That sounds way too scary to me, but since we have flashlights and you're going to stay, I can give you the five-cent tour," Cheryl offered.

"Sure." Guenevere dipped into her messenger bag. Among the emergency flares, miniature first aid kit, EMF meter, holy water and iron nails she found a heavy black flashlight and a smaller version. She handed the heavy one to Janet before flicking on lighter one for herself.

"Wow those are bright." Cheryl commented.

"It saves on tripping," Janet said.

The realtor looked them over. "Well I wouldn't want you to get such nice outfits dirty."

"Oh we have work clothes in the van." Guenevere explained.

Cheryl nodded. "Of course, that makes sense. I guess we can start down here." She turned towards the dining room and frowned at the dining table's web tent. "I can't believe how quickly they come back. I just went through here last week!" She swished the broom through the worst of the web. "I apologize. Once you've declared the place ghost free, I can bring in fumigators and clean the place up. We really want to get this place sold. Your all-clear is a big part of it." She looked up at the webs across the staircase, groaned, and repeated the dusting motion with the broom. The two young women watched her for a moment before Guenevere spoke up. "Chances are the ghosts are something mundane and completely rational. Things like a draft, or an unbalanced door that opens by itself or maybe a defective electrical fixture that is causing lights to flicker." Guenevere said.

"That's probably what it is," Cheryl agreed. "Wind whistling through the gable vents above the tower garret could sound like crying—and if there's a draft…that could easily explain a banging door."

"It could also be mice, or bats, or—" Janet began to suggest.

"No." Cheryl shook her head. "It's not that. I'm very proud to say we've never had critters, not mice, not rats, not bats. Guenevere resisted the urge to voice her doubts. All too often noises in an attic turned out to be bats, raccoons, or squirrels and pest control was needed, not their services. "The tower garret…is that where the weird stuff has been happening?" Guenevere took a half step toward the stairs, gesturing to them.

"Well, I've never heard anything or seen anything but that's where the screaming and banging was supposedly heard."

"By who? Who's hearing it?" Janet asked.

"Hikers and skiers. They wander through the woods and report it to the police and then we get a call to come down and open the place up. They never find anything. I doubt you will either." Cheryl shrugged.

"Like you said, it's probably a draft and the wind whistling." Janet nodded.

"We should probably start there then." Guenevere glanced at Janet who nodded in agreement.

"I like that, straight to business." Cheryl beamed at them. "Well the garret is at the very top. Shall we?"

A noticeable buzz emanating from Cheryl's purse interrupted her. She apologized, starting to lean the broom against the wall before Guenevere took it from her. Expressing a word of thanks, she lifted a mobile phone from her purse, and with a look of surprise, and an apology to the pair, answered it.

Janet and Guenevere tried not to listen in as Cheryl moved down the hall, her voice becoming excited and concerned. She returned a moment later. "Sorry—I seem to be doing a lot of apologizing today. That was the school. My son, Tim, fell and broke his arm—"

Guenevere's face filled with concern. "Oh no! Is he alright?"

"He's going to be fine, but they sent him to the hospital and I have to go and be with him." Her shoulders slumped, "Sorry, you came all the way from the city and it's just one thing after another."

"It's okay," Janet shrugged. "Most of the time the property owners aren't around when we're doing our thing. If you want to leave us the keys, we can lock up, and drop them off."

Cheryl pondered the offer for a second. "Sure…that would work." She pulled the front door key from her purse to hand it over then paused and pulled a jangling ring of nineteen century skeleton keys from her purse. "You'll need these too. I'm not sure which ones are for which doors but they will get you into any room in the house."

Guenevere accepted the keys. "You just take care of Tim, and we'll find our way around."

"Thanks. Again, I'm sorry for running out on you. Just drop the keys off at the office on Main Street and we'll talk later."

"It's okay. We'll be fine." Guenevere reassured her, watching Cheryl scamper out the front door.

After Cheryl was down the steps, Janet spoke up, "Damn it's dark in here."

Guenevere shone her flashlight up the stairs and gazed into the darkness. Her heart fluttered. "Let's…let's leave the front door open,"

Janet nodded. "More light and fresh air that way."

Janet picked up the other broom and gestured to the stairs, "After you, then."

Cautiously they ascended, their footfalls on the creaking steps reverberating through the otherwise, placid house.

"Geez, the dust, and cobwebs!" Janet complained.

"…and the quiet." Guenevere added, peering first left, right down the web shrouded corridor.

Swatting the webs away, they passed several heavy wooden doors bordered by intricate molding; their once dark, shiny surfaces, dulled with dust. Guenevere paused to try one of them. The door's handle rattled as she turned it and the door squeaked inward.

Blacked out from the shuttered and boarded up windows, their flashlight beams quickly found a dusty bed and wardrobe. The bed was unmade, the wardrobe open where dust-caked shirts and trousers hung untouched.

Guenevere felt a sudden sense of sympathy. "They left everything…the family that abandoned the house."

"Yeah…" Janet responded, her tone thoughtful.

Guenevere pulled the door shut and cast her eyes upwards. "Let's go."

The pair ascended to the third floor, pausing to get their bearings. Lifting a red-lacquered nail to her lips, Guenevere looked left then right. "I think it's that door…" She started for end of the hall, trying doors as they walked and finding them locked.

"Maybe to keep them from rattling?" Janet suggested.

Guenevere turned her head to speak. "Well if they're swinging in a draft…"

"Something to check once we get set up." Janet nodded.

The hair on Guenevere's neck prickled as they reached the door at the end of the hall. She felt pins and needles in her palms as they began to sweat. "Ready?" she asked, reaching out to seize the door knob.

"As I'll ever be," Janet responded dryly.

Guenevere tried the door and found it locked. "One of these has to be it…" she said, lifting the ring of skeleton keys and trying one after the next, waiting for a satisfying click. The door opened to a narrow, spiral staircase leading up into the tower garret. A glance at the inner side of the door revealed a tragic scene. The wood around the knob was gouged and scratched. "Oh no…" she pointed, "Look."

Janet's expression softened. "Those poor kids."

Guenevere swallowed a lump in her throat. "They must have been so scared…just terrified. I hope they're still not here, I hope they moved on."

Janet expression became grim. "Let's go find out…"

"Careful the steps are steep," a tiny voice said

Guenevere's hair prickled. "Did you hear that?"

Janet shivered. The skin beneath her blouse goose pimpled, she rubbed her arm reflexively. "Do you feel that?"

"Yes." Guenevere caught sight of her breath. "We need to set up the mic and laptop right away." Guenevere pressed her hand to the stairwell's wood paneling for support and lit the way upward.

"What did you hear?" Janet persisted, following her.

"Careful, the steps are steep.'"

"*I am being* careful." Janet said impatiently, pressing her hand to the wall and following her friend.

The early afternoon sun streamed through a tiny circular window at the top of the ceiling. The light revealed a nursery. A rocking horse occupied a corner, a dollhouse rested upon a short table, a china doll sat in a tiny rocking chair, blocks and toy soldiers lay strewn about the floor.

A sad expression upon her face, Guenevere's hand rose to her throat. She felt Janet's comforting hand upon her shoulder.

"It's so sad…" Guenevere murmured, looking at the remnants of two young lives cut short.

"Let's see if they're here…" Janet suggested.

Guenevere felt the room's temperature drop and shivered. "I think they are. Do you feel…"

"Yeah. Thermal camera?" Janet stretched out her free hand. Guenevere rummaged through her bag. The black satchel contained a mixture of high-tech detection devices, and traditional, some would say archaic, methods of confronting the supernatural. "Here…" she handed off the device.

Janet seized its handle and switched it on to stare at the small infrared screen as she panned across the room. Arriving at the corner closest to the stairs, her jaw dropped open.

"Guen! Look! Look! Look!" Janet pointed frantically at two blue shapes surrounded by greens and yellows on the screen.

"I see them…" The hair on the back of her neck prickling, the blonde ignored the camera as she stared where Janet aimed it.

Sitting in the corner, dressed in nightshirts from another time, sat two little figures, their knees drawn up to their pale, transparent chins. Gaunt, with sunken cheeks and eyes, the apparitions of a little boy and girl starred back at them.

Janet looked up from the camera and gasped. "Oh my God…"

Her mouth suddenly dry, Guenevere licked her lips and spoke. "Tommy? Mary?"

The pair remained silent, holding her gaze with eyes blackened by death.

"Get the…get the laptop set up." Without looking down, Guenevere extended the pocket of her bag for Janet to access it.

"But…right…" Janet said pulling the computer from the bag, along with a microphone.

It seemed an eternity as Janet frantically opened the computer, powered it up, and pulled up an audio program.

"Are you ready?" Guenevere asked, swallowing her fear, the cold of the room forgotten.

"I'm hurrying!" Janet hissed, glancing up from the screen at the pair of tiny ghosts.

"Get your phone too."

"I know!"

Several seconds passed. Guenevere hoped their incredible find would not suddenly vanish.

"Recording!" Janet declared, finding her mobile phone in her purse and lifting and pointing it at the pair.

"Tommy? Mary? Can you hear me?" Guenevere asked, never taking her eyes from the pair.

Janet glanced at the screen app. The recorder's wave form spiked but she heard nothing. "It caught something."

"Can you play it back?"

"Um…" Janet glanced from her phone, to the little ghosts, to the computer's screen. "One sec…"

"*So hungry…*" a soft, plaintive voice sprang from the computer's speaker.

"I'm sorry…" Guenevere crouched down to regard them sympathetically.

Janet watched another wave form spike. "There's more…"

Guenevere kept her eyes on the pair. "Play it back, please…"

"*Mother locked us in because of the monster…*" the tiny voice soft and creaking with fatigue continued.

"Monster?" Guenevere asked.

"Another spike." Janet reported, manipulating the laptop's mouse pad to play it back.

"*In the basement—*" the first voice reported.

"*Run!*" The second one interrupted.

As if a switch had been thrown, the two little figures blinked out of sight.

Guenevere stood up. "Wait! Don't go! Mary? Tommy?" She looked back at Janet. "Are they here?"

Janet picked up the infrared camera and slowly swept the room in a slow circle. "Nothing blue showing up."

"Tommy? Mary?" Guenevere persisted, delving into her bag for an Electromagnetic Field Meter, she quickly switched it on and began scanning the room. "There's no electricity in the house, if they're here…" she watched the needle for signs of a disturbance. Discounting its movement when passing over Janet and their electronics, the instrument detected no sign of the pair.

"Where would they go?"

Janet pressed her lips together, shook her head, and shrugged.

Guenevere lowered the EMF meter. "Probably not the basement, which is why we have to go down there."

"The basement? Something that scares ghosts and you want to confront it?"

"Investigate. Do you realize what a great episode this would make? And those two kids need to be with their family. They've suffered enough."

"I think we should go home, call Monsignor Mike and see what he thinks."

"Thinks about what? Ask for an exorcism when we don't even know if there's anything there?"

"Let me get my gun then." Janet said.

"If it's an entity, it's useless."

"This is getting very weird."

"All the real ones are. Come on Janet…*two*…two!"

Guenevere held up two fingers, "Type one, fully interactive personalities; that's practically unheard of! We're going to be investigative legends!" Guenevere grinned.

Janet eyed her friend dubiously.

Guenevere regarded her impatiently. "Come on! Let's pack up and find the basement. We've stumbled onto something big." She began to close down the laptop and wind up the microphone's cord.

"I'd rather not stumble…" Janet murmured, depositing her mobile phone back into her purse.

"Let's go…" Guenevere implored, motioning for Janet to follow her.

Retracing their steps through the blackness of the house, Guenevere held her EMF meter before her and called out the children's names hoping for another manifestation. Back on the main floor, she set it aside as they tried every door before finding a set of stairs off the kitchen.

They stood in the darkness, looking at each other by the beams of their flashlights.

"Are you sure about this?" Janet asked.

"Yes…just one sec…" Guenevere pointed the EMF meter at the cellar. The needle remained motionless. "Nothing." She shrugged and clattered down the stairs.

Standing at the foot of the stairs, Guenevere's nose wrinkled, she struggled to suppress a high-pitched sneeze. "Oh geez…" She waved a hand in front of her nose futilely attempting to wave the scent of mould and damp earth from her nose. "It's worse here…"

Janet coughed and nodded, widening her flashlight's beam to swing across the cellar's expanse before settling on a set of stairs and a pair of bulkhead doors secured with a chain and padlock. "Do you think…" she paused to wrinkle her nose, "…we could open those?"

"We're going to…" Guenevere dipped into her bag to exchange her EMF meter and flashlight for a slender black pouch the size of her palm. She approached the doors, "Can you...? Thanks." She said as Janet focused the flashlight on the padlock.

Janet watched the blonde extract two gleaming tools from the pouch. "My grandpa would have something to say about your lock picking."

"Locksmithing." Guenevere's expression became one of concentration. She carefully inserted one of the slender tools into the padlock pressing it down while turning and manipulating the other. After a few seconds, the lock popped open. She quickly pulled the chain away and pushed the doors open allowing fresh air and the afternoon's sunshine to flood the cellar.

"Oh wow that's bright." Guenevere blinked.

Janet inhaled deeply. "Much better." Leaving her light on she swept it across the cellar. "Nothing down here but shelves, dusty canning jars, and cob-webs."

"Maybe…" Guenevere bit her bottom lip in thought. "Cheryl said this was a station on the Underground Railroad. That means freedom seekers would have been hidden here."

"And?"

"Didn't you take American history?"

"In grade 9…"

Guenevere resisted the urge to sigh. Her studies of the paranormal often required a keen knowledge of history. Janet's strengths lay elsewhere. "It means these places sometimes had concealed rooms or a sub-basement. Look for a secret door." Guenevere began tapping on the walls with the butt of her flashlight. "It will sound hollow." Janet frowned but obliged her. She started at the stone walls of the exterior and moved inward to tap her flashlight against the interior wooden wall. Guenevere did likewise starting beside the stairs leading to the kitchen, and moving around the wall towards Janet.

 After several moments, Janet's rapping became a hollow thump. She paused, repeating the gesture before continuing for several inches and receiving a similar sound.

"Did you find something?" Guenevere asked.

Janet shrugged. "I don't know, but it's a different sound." Guenevere strode purposefully across the floor, an excitement welling in her belly. "Let me try…" She repeated Janet's rapping and received the same hollow thump. Her gaze darted around the area. She pushed and pressed on the boards, tugged at cross members, and ran her nimble fingers along the dusty wood. "There has to be a latch, a release, a switch of some kind."

"Should I go get the tool box? I can bring the van around." Janet glanced at the set of stairs leading up through the bulkhead doors leading outside.

Guenevere reached up and tugged the cross member above their heads. Attached to a cord, set into the ceiling, the board separated from its surroundings. A section of the wall cracked open a finger width. Her eyes gleamed. "Found it."

She pressed on the door. It barely moved. Gritting her teeth, she pushed with both hands and cringed as rusted hinges groaned before giving way.

Janet came alongside her. "Probably hasn't been opened in a hundred years."

"And then some…" Guenevere looked down at brown dust on her hands and rubbed them together. Janet handed her a bottle of hand sanitizer to speed up her efforts.

Heart racing, Guenevere peered inward and examined the passage beyond first by the ambient light streaming in from outside before switching on her flashlight. "Wow…" she marveled. "I'll bet we're the first people to see this since the Civil War."

"I'll see if I can negotiate for a higher fee for this," Janet said over Guenevere's shoulder.

Guenevere shot her a look of annoyance. She retrieved the broom to begin to swat away the dusty cobwebs hanging across the passage.

"What do you see?" Janet asked, peeking out from behind her friend.

Guenevere handed the broom back to her. "Another door…" She shone her light on it.

"So what's behind the door?"

Guenevere switched back to her EMF meter and held it up before her. "According to this…nothing resembling a monster. Let's go see anyway…" Guenevere gave her a mischievous smile, and started forward.

Janet rolled her eyes.

Lifting the simple latch, the door swung inward to musty moth-eaten straw pallets, a rough hewn table and chairs, and another door. Carved upon it was a circle with seven blunt petals stretching outward.

"What's that mean?" Janet point.

Guenevere shook her head. "I don't remember anything like that in history class. Maybe it's a sun, a sign of hope." Guenevere shrugged and paused to snap a picture with her mobile device. She would identify it later.

Janet groaned at the sudden flash.

Guenevere glanced at her and apologized before reaching for the door's iron latch.

"Meter?" Janet asked staring at the door.

"Thanks for reminding me…" Guenevere found the device and watched the needle for any signs of motion."Nothing…" Shrugging, Guenevere replaced the meter in her bag and depressed the door's latch, grunting as she found it stuck. They pulled on it together. It scraped across the stone floor and shuddered open.

The shone their lights inside and found a narrow passage, barely wide enough for a man's shoulders. The walls the hidden room and the passage to it were constructed of fieldstone. This passage was rough, grey, craggy, crudely mined with pick and chisel out of the bedrock upon which the house rested.

"Not a good place for claustrophobics…" Janet murmured.

"Do you think it's an escape tunnel? In case the room was discovered?" Guenevere asked.

"I don't know." Janet shrugged.

"I want to see where it goes." Guenevere started forward, holding her light before her.

"Why don't we get the gear?" Janet asked.

Guenevere shone the light up to the ceiling. Like the walls and floor it was rough hewn. "Just bring the broom in case we find more webs."

"Or monsters." Janet said, wryly.

"I suppose." Guenevere said before venturing forward with Janet in tow.

The passage continued for several steps before winding left to crudely made steps, some were broad and shallow, others steep and narrow.

"Careful." Guenevere instructed over her shoulder.

"You want to go down them in heels?" Janet crouched to peek past her friend at their path.

"If it gets too bad, we'll turn back."

"Famous last words…"

Guenevere frowned. Sometimes her friend's cynicism irked her. "Come on. We get to do things that other people only dream of."

"I think the word you want is nightmare, and I'd rather be in work boots."

"If you want to, go back and change, but I'm going to keep going."

"Fine." Janet followed, watching as Guenevere braced her free hand on the rock wall for balance and carefully negotiated her way down.

They arrived at a small landing where the nub of a candle rested in a niche in the wall. A trail of candle wax trickled down the wall towards the floor. The air was noticeably cooler here, like a crisp autumn evening.

Guenevere paused to use her meter and found no electromagnetic presence. She put the temperature change down to the natural subterranean atmosphere and moved on.

"How far down do you think we are?" Guenevere asked absently.

Janet turned back and shined her light on the steps to count them. "Fifteen steps, close to a storey."

"There's another door at the bottom." Guenevere continued forward, feeling her heart racing in anticipation.

"Probably not an escape tunnel." Janet said.

"Not sure what it is." Guenevere said, her hand trailing along the wall as she negotiated the stairwell, with some steps so narrow that they were forced to step sideways.

"Let's get the gear."

Guenevere started down the stairs. "You go ahead. I'll be fine."

Janet frowned and carefully started back up the stairs.
Guenevere considered the door, shifted and her flashlight's
beam from it to her next step and back again.

Reaching the foot of the stairs she shone her light on the
plank door. It had the carving as the upper door. She
paused and snapped another picture before lifting the
wooden latch and pushing the door inward.

Wheezing coughs erupted from her throat as the musty air
threatened to overwhelm her. She groaned, and swallowed.
She shone the light upwards to the passage's ceiling in
search of bats. Seeing none, she directed the light down the
narrow passage and found spider webs; some so thick they
resembled ragged, dusty bandages.

Guenevere pressed her lips together in thought before
dipping into her bag. For a moment she juggled her
flashlight and a road flare before swapping the flashlight for
the flare. Her path illuminated by the flare's brilliance, but
much shorter range, Guenevere moved forward. The webs
hissed and crackled as she lifted the flare to them, burning
her way deeper into the passage.

A pause to check the EMF meter yielded no indications of
ghosts. Exploring gave her a delicious thrill. The clicking
and scraping of her heels echoed softly off the rocky walls.
Carefully, cautiously, Guenevere crept forward. She spared
frequent glances at the cavern's uneven floor and
reluctantly wondered if Janet had been right about boots
over heels in this place. The flare's light was brilliant but

unfocused, its glare interfered with her ability to see far ahead. Her belly fluttered with nervous excitement, her skin goose-pimpled and her palms prickled.

She was the first person seeing this place in over a hundred and fifty years, it alone could make for a documentary. She pondered contacting her agent about negotiating the legal rights to do it. Licking her lips and taking a steadying breath, she moved on.

A shape manifested in the gloom. As she drew closer she realized the passage was opening up to something larger. The shape dimensions became clearer; it was flat, waist-high, and constructed of the same stone that made up the passage. She gave the floor another glance for obstacles and quickened her pace.

The flare's light illuminated a round chamber. At its center lay a long flat stone with the same symbol as the door, carved into its side. The walls were smooth, polished, and covered in pictograms. Holding up her mobile device, its flash illuminated the chamber with the brightness of a lightning strike. She rapidly snapped multiple pictures before turning to the pictograms.

Consisting of stick figures, dots, and geometric shapes, the pictograms began at the floor and continued upwards. Fascinated, she traced their outlines with her fingers. Her gaze rose. She tilted her head back to gain sight of it all.

A gasp escaped her lips. Dusty, human shaped, silk cocoons hung from the ceiling. From the darkness came a high-pitched screech.

A child screamed, *"Watch out!"*

Adrenaline shot through Guenevere's veins as a dark aberration launched from among the cocoons, its long gangly arms extended towards her.

She screamed and ducked as the purplish-grey thing swished her overhead.

Guenevere spun reflexively to find it.

Clinging to the wall, its four limbs ending in twin thick claws was something out of a nightmare. Bulbous and thick bodied, its head was that of a spider, eight glittering black eyes, with broad mandibles that clacked together as if mocking her.

Screaming again, Guenevere turned to run.

She stumbled into the altar and grunted.

The fiend launched itself again. It landed behind her.

She wheeled, attempting to get past it and escape.

It blocked her path, screeching and grasping her arm. Her mobile clattered to the floor.

Guenevere's heart raced. She swung the flare like a weapon.

The thing swatted her wrist and sending the light flying.

She strained against the grip on her arm. The sleeve of her blouse tore.

It's free hand came down on her scalp, pushing her head to the side and lunging in with its gaping mandibles. Two hypodermic fangs extended from its black mouth and stabbed into the flesh between her neck and shoulder. Venom flowed into her veins. White hot pain creased her features.

Guinevere felt weak. Dizzy. Her mind screamed to run, to fight, to escape, but her legs refused to move. She was falling, and spinning...

Spinning...

Spinning…

# # #

"Guenevere! Guen!" Janet called. She reached the bottom of the crude stairwell, set down a heavy plastic case, and shrugged off a backpack full of lights, sensors, and other technical gear. Her mining helmet's light illuminated her surroundings. She wore a set of red coveralls striped with bands of yellow and white reflective tape. Gone were the heels, replaced by sturdy work boots. Around her waist was an army surplus belt complete with a canteen, a heavy black flashlight, a Leatherman multi-tool, and a holster containing her grandfather's pistol.

Passing through the door, she repeated herself.

"Guenevere!"

The distant glow of a flare drew her attention. Sighing, she started down the corridor, feeling the tightness of its confines as she moved deeper into the subterranean cavern.

"Did you find—" she cut her question short. Guenevere's messenger bag lay on the ground, its shoulder strap torn. Heart in her throat, Janet blinked and recalled the child-ghost's warning about monsters. Her hand strayed to her revolver, jerking it free of its holster. She advanced cautiously, her head on a swivel, straining to hear, forcing herself to halt her ragged breaths. "Guenevere?" she called softly.

Hearing nothing, she advanced purposefully. Her pulse pounded her ears. Her knuckles whitened around the gun's grip. "Guenevere, where are you?" she asked desperate to hear an answer.

Finding the chamber Janet scanned the scene. One of her friend's shoes lay at her booted feet, the other lay nearby next to the stone altar. A red road flare blazed away next to the wall.

Frantic, Janet looked to the other six passages branching off from the center. Frustrated, she tipped her head back to bellow Guenevere's name and gasped at what she saw.

Dusty, human shaped web cocoons—including a new one, fresh, white, and distinctly female in shape. Suspended high off the ground, it hung motionless. Her gut clenched with fear.

"Guenevere!" Janet cried, beginning to climb the altar in an attempt to reach her.

A screech from behind set her hair on end. She turned to see a monstrous shape, bounding out of the darkness ape-like on all fours.

Instinctively she fired her pistol from the hip, emptying its cylinder into her charging attacker.

Pop-pop-pop-pop-pop-pop.

Her fusillade echoed through the cavern.

Like a spider touched by a flame, the monstrosity seized and trembled before screeching again. Sickly green wounds appeared on its thorax, pouring forth its blood. Relentless, it continued its charge.

Janet hurled the revolver at it.

The attack was batted aside.

Wide-eyed, Janet desperately looked for a weapon. Her eyes found the flare, still blazing on the stone floor. She dove for it.

The monster entered the chamber, and launched itself at its prey.

Seizing the flare, Janet spun onto her back, and teeth bared, bellowed a challenge. She thrust the flare before her like a rapier. She caught the thing between its mandibles, cramming the blazing flare into its maw.

An acrid stench filled the chamber.

The fiend reared back and clawed at its mouth, as the intense heat boiled its blood and burned through to its brain.

Janet rolled to one side and regained her feet as the creature thrashed about, its brains crackling and popping as it burned. She dashed for her pistol while pawing at her pocket for its extra bullets.

With trembling hands she snapped the revolver open, dumped the spent brass and began to reload. She cast repeated fearful glances at her assailant then saw it go still. A child's tiny sigh filled the chamber, followed by a yawn. *"You got rid of the monster."*

A second one joined it. *"Thank you. Time to sleep…"*

Still clutching the weapon, Janet scrambled up onto the altar, grunting as she jumped in a failed attempt to reach Guenevere's suspended form.

"Guenevere!" she called, her eyes becoming moist. Jumping down, she picked up Guenevere's mobile device, attempting a 9-1-1 call before cursing at the lack of reception.

"Hold on! Just hold on! I'm going to get help!" She hesitated sparing her friend a quick glance before sprinting for the stairs.

# # #

With Janet at the wheel, and Guenevere's left arm in a sling, the two of them passed a bevy of official vehicles from state, local, and federal law enforcement and various health and environmental agencies. Their unexpected find had turned the Monahan house into a hive of activity. A line of yellow police tape surrounded the acreage. Heavily armed state and local law enforcement combed the woods for any further traces of bodies or examples of what they found hidden beneath the house.

Guenevere pressed her lips together in a grimace. Despite the pain killers and the sling, her left side from neck to wrist continued to throb. A treatment called Antivenin administered at the hospital neutralized the spider venom and revived her to consciousness, but the deep bruising of her muscles remained.

Guenevere ducked her head to regard Cheryl in the passenger side mirror. As they drove from their brief meeting with the realtor, the figure shrank with each passing second. "I feel sorry for her."

Janet glanced over at her friend from the driver's seat. "We didn't create this mess."

"True." Guenevere shrugged, then winced. "We, well, *you* ended the worst part of it." She looked over at Janet. "But you found it."

"Remind me never to do something like that again." Janet struggled not to roll her eyes in disbelief at the request.

"What?" Guenevere asked, seeing the expression.

"Nothing…" Janet shook her head, struggling not to smirk. "What!"

Janet watched the road.

Guenevere frowned, her face creasing peevishly.

"Do you think we were right not to tell her it was a…a—"

"A Mmuo ojoo udide?" Guinevere named the mystical monster that, until the previous day, was merely a West African myth. Her telephone call to Professor Arnold Jefferson, her mentor at Princeton, sent him combing tomes for something matching its description and circumstance.

"Yeah."

Guenevere grimaced. "They just found the remains of twenty people under that house. I think letting her believe it was just a big spider is enough."

"At least those two kids are free. Haunting terminated."

Guen grimaced with disappointment. "I doubt they'll let us tell this story."

"If anyone would even ever believe it."

"You're probably right" Guenevere conceded.

"If I see a gas station we'll stop so we can get some more ice for your shoulder."

"Thanks." Guenevere looked over at Janet appreciatively.

<u>Thank you</u>

Thank you for reading my book. If you enjoyed the story, please consider leaving an honest review at the site of purchase.

About the Author

Born and raised in a rural community in Ontario, Canada, and practically living in the classics section of the children's library, Lance began writing tales of adventure and heroism in the fourth grade. An old soul, he tries to sing, and dance, and play, a little each day. He has degrees in political science and psychology.

Check out his webpage: www.jlmeredith.com for announcements, contests, or to read his blog.

Facebook Page Address:
https://www.facebook.com/JLMWrites/

Twitter/X: https://x.com/JLM_Writes

www.ingramcontent.com/pod-product-compliance
Lightning Source LLC
Chambersburg PA
CBHW040527170726
48295CB00012B/373